THE SECRETARY'S SCANDALOUS SECRET

BY
CATHY WILLIAMS

All the   agination
of the a   g the
same na   ny
individual known or unknown to the author, and all the incidents are
pure invention.

All Rights Reserved including the right of reproduction in whole or
in part in any form. This edition is published by arrangement with
Harlequin Enterprises II BV/S.à.r.l. The text of this publication or
any part thereof may not be reproduced or transmitted in any form
or by any means, electronic or mechanical, including photocopying,
recording, storage in an information retrieval system, or otherwise,
without the written permission of the publisher.

This book is sold subject to the condition that it shall not, by way of
trade or otherwise, be lent, resold, hired out or otherwise circulated
without the prior consent of the publisher in any form of binding or
cover other than that in which it is published and without a similar
condition including this condition being imposed on the subsequent
purchaser.

® and TM are trademarks owned and used by the trademark owner
and/or its licensee. Trademarks marked with ® are registered with the
United Kingdom Patent Office and/or the Office for Harmonisation in
the Internal Market and in other countries.

First published in Great Britain 2011
Harlequin Mills & Boon Limited,
Eton House, 18-24 Paradise Road, Richmond, Surrey TW9 1SR

© Cathy Williams 2011

ISBN: 978 0 263 88624 5

Harlequin Mills & Boon policy is to use papers that are natural,
renewable and recyclable products and made from wood grown in
sustainable forests. The logging and manufacturing process conform
to the legal environmental regulations of the country of origin.

Printed and bound in Spain
by Litografia Rosés, S.A., Barcelona

THE SECRETARY'S SCANDALOUS SECRET

CHAPTER ONE

'I CALLED. Five minutes ago. You failed to pick up.' Luc Laughton flicked back the cuff of his shirt to look pointedly at his watch. 'I don't appreciate clock-watching in my employees. People who work for me are well paid for a reason.'

Cool green eyes swept over the small blonde huddled in a thick coat of indeterminate colour that looked as though it had been rescued from the local charity shop. There was, he was forced to concede, a pretty good chance that it had been, knowing her as he did.

Bright patches of colour had appeared on Agatha's cheeks. Of course she had heard the telephone ring. Of course she had known that she really *should* have picked it up—but she had been in a rush, and it wasn't as though she didn't put in her fair share of overtime when it was necessary. In fact, it was already five-forty-five, so it was hardly as though she had raced to join the five o'clock Friday-evening exodus!

'Because you're here as a favour to my mother,' Luc continued with that implacable edge of steel in his voice that made him so feared in the cut-throat world of high finance, 'doesn't mean that you can slope off on the dot of five whenever it suits you.'

'It's after five-thirty, and I wasn't sloping off.' Agatha stared down at the ground with ferocious concentration because it was a lot less traumatic than actually having to look at Luc Laughton. Looking at Luc Laughton always resulted in a thumping heart, a racing pulse and an inconvenient, prickly feeling all over her body. It had been that way since she had been a kid of thirteen and he had been eighteen—on the verge of manhood, fabulously good-looking and with the sort of dangerous, dark looks that made women stop and stare and then do a double-take every time he walked by.

How could she have failed to have a crush? All the girls in the village had had a crush on him, not that he had ever paid any of them a blind bit of notice. He was the rich kid who lived in the mansion on the hill. He had attended a top boarding school which had honed his razor-sharp intellect and invested him with the kind of cool self-assurance that Agatha had found both scary and weirdly compelling.

'If it's important, I guess I could stay on a bit longer...' she mumbled to the carpet.

Luc gave an elaborate sigh and leaned against the door frame. He had known from the very beginning that this was where the favour to his mother would end up, but what choice had he been given?

Six years ago his father had died unexpectedly, leaving behind him a financial train-wreck brought about by gross mismanagement of his company by the person he had most trusted. While Luc had been living it up at university, on the verge of leaving for Harvard to begin a Masters in economics and history, the wealth that had supported a lifestyle way beyond most people's wildest dreams had been unravelling faster than the speed of light. His charming father had played golf and entertained clients, and his unscrupulous finance director had played with the books and embezzled vast sums of money.

Luc had been summoned home to face a grief-stricken

mother and a house about to go under the hammer to pay off the creditors who had been baying like wolves at the door.

Distraught at having nowhere to live, Danielle had been taken in by the vicar and his wife. They had looked after her and seen her through some tough times for the better part of a year, until the misery of her non-existent finances had been sorted. Sufficient money had been scraped together to rent a small cottage outside the village, which had provided her with a roof over her head while Luc had abandoned his postgrad plans and begun the process of savagely, ruthlessly and single-mindedly reclaiming what had been lost.

So when, eight months ago, his mother had told him that little Agatha Havers had been made redundant a few months ago and needed a job he had had no option but to provide one. Her parents had been an invaluable rock to his mother when she had most needed one, and thanks to them he had had the freedom to instigate the meteoric rise which, less than four years later, would see his mother restored to the house that was rightfully hers.

In the high-tech glass building with its high-achieving staff, however, Agatha stood out like a sore thumb. The daughter of the local vicar of a small parish in a small village in the middle of nowhere, trained in the vital skills of gardening and potting plants, was perilously out of step in his world of mergers, acquisitions and making money.

'Has Helen gone?' Helen was Luc's personal assistant. Agatha felt sorry for her. *She* might get bits and pieces of his eagle-eyed attention, but Helen received the full brunt of it, because Luc was nothing if not an exacting task-master. Agatha could only shudder at the thought of having to be under Luc's radar all day, only to return home to all the peace and quiet of four children and a husband.

'She has. Not that that's relevant. I need you to collate the information on the Garsi deal and then make sure that all the legal documents are in order. The schedule is tight on this one, so it's all hands to the deck.'

'Wouldn't you be better off…um…getting someone a little more experienced to deal with something like that?' Agatha ventured hesitantly.

Unable to continue staring at the carpet any longer, she reluctantly looked up at him and instantly she felt as though the oxygen levels had plummeted as she feverishly absorbed the refined, beautiful angles of his face. He had inherited the olive skin and black hair from his French mother, and the green eyes of his very English, very aristocratic father, and they worked together to give him drop-dead, killer looks.

'I'm not asking you to seal the deal, Agatha.'

'I realise that, but I'm not as fast on the computer as, well…'

'Most people in the building?' Luc inserted helpfully, fighting to keep the sarcasm out of his voice. 'You've had nearly eight months to get to grips with the work and you apparently did a one-month crash course in IT.'

Agatha tried not to shudder at the memory of that particular course. Having been made redundant from the garden centre, she had spent three months at home with her mother and, sweet-natured though her mother was, she knew that her patience had been tried to the limit.

'You can't spend the rest of your days drifting through the house and tinkering in the garden, darling,' she had said gently. 'I love having you here, especially since your dad passed on two years ago, but you need a job. If you don't think that there are any jobs around here, well, why don't you perhaps think of working further afield? Maybe even London? I've had a little word with Danielle, Luc's mother, and she suggested that Luc might be able to find a spot for you in his company. He's very successful, you know—does something important in the City. All you'd need to do would be a short little computer course…'

Agatha privately thought that most ten-year-old kids had more computer savvy than her, but then computers had not been much in evidence in the vicarage. By the time she'd emerged into a world reliant on them, she had found herself wildly at sea and woefully ignorant. Computers, for her, were not friends to be played with. They were potential enemies out to get the better of her the second she pressed a wrong key.

'Yes, I did,' she said glumly. 'But I really wasn't brilliant at it.'

'You'll never get anywhere in life if you droop around convinced that failure lies just around the corner. I'm giving you a golden opportunity to take a step up from filing.'

'I don't mind filing,' Agatha said quickly. 'I mean, I know it's dull, but I never expected to…'

'To find working here exciting?' Luc held on to his patience with difficulty. Agatha, as timid as a mouse, and as background as canned elevator-music, irritated him. He could remember her as a teenager, skulking in corners, too tongue-tied to hold even the most basic of conversations with him. Apparently she was absolutely fine with everyone else, or so his mother had assured him. He had his doubts. Right now, she was trying hard to disappear into the folds of her oversized coat.

'Well?' he demanded impatiently.

'I don't think I'm really cut out for office work,' honesty compelled her to admit. 'Not that I'm not incredibly grateful for the opportunity to work here…' Or at least, she thought realistically, the opportunity to occupy a broom cupboard on the third floor from where she typed the occasional letter and received orders to file the occasional file. Mostly she was at his beck and call to do such things as sort out his dry cleaning, ensure his fridge was well stocked for those fleeting occasions when he was going to be in his apartment in Belgravia and see off his discarded women with appropriate tokens of fond farewell, ranging from lots of flowers to diamonds—a job delegated to her by Helen. In the space of eight months, five exotic supermodels had been given the red card.

'I realise you probably didn't have much of a choice.'

'None at all,' Luc agreed deflatingly. Nervous though she was, it would have been terrific if he had contradicted her statement, perhaps told her that she was, in her own way, a valued member of staff.

'Yes, Danielle and Mum can be quite forceful when they put their minds to it.'

'Agatha, why don't you sit down for a few minutes? I should have had a little chat with you sooner, but time's in scarce supply for me.'

'I know.' She hovered indecisively for a few seconds, then reluctantly shuffled back to her desk and sat down, watching as Luc perched on the edge and subjected her to one of those blistering looks that promised unwelcome revelations—probably to do with her lack of computer skills, or at the very least at her lack of enthusiasm for developing what precious few computer skills she did have.

Distracted, Luc frowned. 'What do you mean, *you know*?'

'I mean your mum always goes on about how hard you work and how you're never at home.'

Luc could scarcely credit what he was hearing. 'You're telling me that you sit around like the three witches in Macbeth, yakking about me?'

'No! Of course not.'

'Don't you have any kind of life back there? Anything better to do with your time?'

'Of course I have a life!' Or at least she had until she'd been made redundant from the garden centre. Or was he talking about her social life? 'I have lots of friends. You know, not everyone thinks that it's a top priority to head down to London at the first chance and make a fortune.'

'It's just as well I did, though, isn't it?' he inserted silkily. 'In case you'd forgotten, my mother was languishing in a two-bedroom cottage with peeling wallpaper and threadbare carpets. I think you'll agree that someone had to take charge and restore the family finances.'

'Yes.' She stared down at her fingers and then sneaked a look at him, and for a few heart-stopping seconds their eyes clashed, clear blue against deep, mossy green. That crush, which she had done her utmost to kill off, fluttered just below the surface, reminding her that, however hard she looked, Luc Laughton remained in a league of his own. Even when, like now, he was looking at her with the sort of rampant impatience that was even more insulting than open antagonism.

Her ready capitulation made him scowl. 'This...' he spread an expressive hand to encompass the office and beyond '...is real life, and thanks to it my mother can enjoy the lifestyle to which she has always been accustomed. My father made a lot of mistakes when it came to money, and fortunately I have learnt from all of them. Lesson number one is that nothing is achieved without putting in the hours.' He stood up and prowled through the tiny office, which was tucked away from the rest of the offices—and just as well, because he figured that she would have been even more lost had she been positioned in the middle of one of the several buzzing, high-energy floors occupied by his various staff.

'If you're not enjoying your job as much as you'd like, then you only have yourself to blame. Try looking at it as more than just biding time until some other gardening job comes available.'

'I'm not on the look out for another gardening job.' There were none to be had in London. She had looked.

'Take one step towards really integrating in this environment, Agatha. I don't want you to be offended by what I'm about to say…'

'Then don't say it!' She looked at him with big, blue pleading eyes. She knew that he was one of the 'cruel to be kind' breed of person with almost zero tolerance for anyone who didn't take the bull by the horns and wrestle life into subservience like him.

'He can be a little scary,' Danielle had confessed just before Agatha had moved to London. Just how scary, Agatha hadn't realised until she had started working for him. There was little direct contact, because most of her work came via Helen, who always wore a smile and pointed to any inaccuracies in her typing with a kindly shrug. On those occasions when he had descended from his ivory tower and cornered her himself, he had been a lot less forgiving.

'You can't be an ostrich, Agatha.' He paused in his restless, unnerving prowling to stand directly in front of her and waited until he had one-hundred percent of her attention. 'If you had taken your head out of the sand, you would have predicted your redundancy from that garden centre. They'd been losing money for at least two years; the credit crunch was the final straw. You could have been looking for a replacement job instead of waiting until the axe fell and finding yourself on the scrap heap.'

A rare spark of mutiny swept through her and she tightened her lips.

'But, no matter. You're here, and you are being paid a handsome wage, which you earn by taking absolutely no interest in anything at all.'

'I'll try harder,' she muttered, wondering how she could find someone so intensely attractive and yet loathe him at the same time. Were her feelings born out of habit—was that it? A silly, teenaged crush that had developed into some kind of low-lying, semi-permanent virus?

'Yes, you will, and you can start with your choice of clothes.'

'I beg your pardon?'

'I'm telling you this for your own good,' he imparted in the kind of voice that warned her that, whatever he had to say, it definitely wouldn't feel as though it was being delivered for her own good. 'Your choice of clothing doesn't really strike the right note for someone working in these offices. Look around you—do you see anyone one else who dresses in long gypsy skirts and baggy cardigans?'

Agatha was engulfed in a wave of anger and shame. He might be beautiful, but then roses were beautiful until you got to the thorns. How could she have nursed an inappropriate crush on this guy for all these years? she asked herself, not for the first time. From afar, when she'd been a kid, he had appeared all-powerful and so breathtakingly gorgeous. Even when Danielle had moved in with her parents, and she had had a chance to see the three-dimensional Luc when he had visited and stayed, she had still not been put off by the way he had always managed to eliminate her even when she had been right there in his line of vision.

She wasn't a stunning blonde with legs up to her armpits and big hair; it was as simple as that. She was invisible to him, a nondescript nobody who hovered in the periphery, helping prepare suppers and losing herself in the garden.

But he had always been scrupulously polite, even if he had barely registered her growing from a girl to a woman.

This, however, was beyond the pale.

'I'm comfortable in these clothes,' she told him in a

shaking voice. 'And I know you're doing me a huge favour by employing me, when I obviously have no talent for office work, but I don't see why I can't wear what I want. No one important sees me. I don't attend any meetings. And, if you don't mind, I really would like to go now. I have a very important date, as it happens, so if you'll excuse me…?' She stood up.

'A date? You have a *date*?' Luc was startled enough to find himself temporarily sidetracked.

'There's no need to sound so surprised.' Agatha walked towards the door, conscious of his eyes boring into her back.

'I'm surprised because you've been in London all of five minutes. Does Edith know about this?'

'Mum doesn't have to know every single thing I do here!' But she flushed guiltily. Her mother was a firm believer in the gentle art of courtship. She would have had a seizure had she known that her little girl was about to go out for dinner with a guy she had met casually in a bar whilst out with some of her girlfriends. She wouldn't understand that that was just how it happened in London, and she definitely wouldn't understand how important this date was for Agatha. At long last, she had decided to throw herself into the dating scene. Dreamy, fictitious relationships were all well and good for a kid of fifteen; at twenty-two, they were insane. She needed a real relationship with a real man who made real plans for a real future.

'Wait, wait, wait—not so fast, Agatha.' He reached out, captured her arm in a vice-like grip and swivelled her to face him.

'Okay, I'll come in really early tomorrow morning—even though it's Saturday—and sort out that stuff…' Just feeling his long fingers pressing into her coat was bringing her out in nervous perspiration and suddenly, more than ever, she wanted this date. She was sick to death with the way her body reacted to him. 'But I really, really need to get back to my flat or else I'm going to be late for Stewart.'

'Stewart? That the name of the man?' He released her, but his curiosity was piqued by this sudden insight into her private life. He really hadn't thought that she had one. In actual fact, he hadn't thought about her at all, despite his mother's pressing questions whenever he had called, asking him whether she was all right. He had given her a job, made sure that she was paid very well indeed, given her lack of experience, and frankly considered his duty done.

'Yes,' Agatha conceded reluctantly.

'And how long has this situation been going on?'

'I don't see that that's any of your business,' she mumbled with considerable daring. Was she supposed to hang around? Did he still want her to carry on working?

She decided to brave an exit, but she was sickeningly aware of him following her out of her office towards the lift. It was Friday and most of the employees on her floor had already left. She knew that the rest of his dedicated, richly rewarded staff further up the hierarchy would be beavering away, making things happen.

'None of my business? Did I just hear right?'

'Yes, you did.' Frustrated, Agatha swung round to look at him, her hands clenched into tight fists in the spacious pockets of her coat. 'Of course, it's your business what I do here between the hours of nine and whatever time I leave, but whatever I do outside working hours isn't your concern.'

'I wish I could concur but, like it or not, I have a responsibility towards you.'

'Because of a favour my parents did for Danielle a hundred years ago? That's crazy! Dad is—*was*—a vicar. Looking after the parishioners was what he did, and he enjoyed doing it. So did my mother. Not to mention that your mum was already a friend and had helped out countless times at the church fetes.' She punched the lift button and stared at it, ignoring the man at her side.

'Baking a few cakes now and again is a bit different from housing someone for a year.'

'Not for my parents. And Mum would be appalled if she thought that I was in London being a nuisance.' She had to cross her fingers behind her back when she said that. Her mother worried daily about her. Her phone calls were punctuated with anxious questions about her diet, rapidly followed up by not-too-subtle reminders that London was a very dangerous place. Sometimes, to back this up, Edith would quote from newspaper clippings, overblown, dramatic stories about knifings, murders or muggings that had occurred somewhere in London. She was unfailingly sceptical about any reassurances that Agatha was well and fine and didn't live anywhere remotely close to where said knifings or murders or muggings had occurred. Her mother would have loved nothing better than to think that Luc was taking Agatha's welfare on board.

The lift had finally decided to arrive and she looked at Luc in alarm as he stepped inside it with her.

'What…What are you doing?'

'I'm taking the lift down with you.'

'But you can't!'

'How do you work that one out?'

'You've just told me that you have this deal to complete—remember? All hands on deck?' She was about to press the 'ground' button, but Luc got there before her, and she spun round to face him in angry disbelief,

'Why are we going down to the basement?'

'Because my car is there, and I'm giving you a lift to your house.'

'Are you mad?'

'Look, do you want the truth?'

Agatha, in receipt of various home truths from him already, was heartily against hearing any more, but her mouth refused to work.

'I had my mother on the telephone yesterday,' Luc imparted bluntly. 'It would seem that I haven't shown sufficient interest in what you've been up to since you've come here.'

This was turning out to be a favour that carried a very high price. Normally indifferent to the opinions of other people, Luc dearly loved his mother, and so had gritted his teeth and listened in silence as she'd gently quizzed him about Agatha. She'd registered concern when told that he hadn't the faintest idea how she was doing. Nor had she bought in to the logic that he had fulfilled his part of the bargain and so what was the problem if he washed his hands of the problem?

Agatha gaped at him, mortified, barely noticing when the lift doors pinged open and he guided her out of the lift towards a gleaming, silver Aston Martin.

'I don't believe you,' she said in a tight, breathless voice.

'Well, you'd better start. Edith is worried. You don't sound happy; you're vague when she asks you about the job. You tell her that it's all right, by which she takes it to mean that it's making you miserable. The last time she saw you, you seemed to be losing weight.' As far as Luc could make out, under the shapeless coat she looked perfectly healthy to him.

Agatha groaned and buried her head in her hands.

'Strap up and tell me where you live.'

While he fiddled with his sat nav, giving it instructions to go to the address she could barely impart through gritted teeth, Agatha had time to conduct a quick mental review of the last hour, starting with his sudden interest in producing more challenging work for her to do.

'This is awful.' She placed cool hands on her burning cheeks.

'You're telling me.'

'Is that why you hunted me down to give me all that stuff to do?'

'Try getting one-hundred percent involved and you might have less time to spend crying down the line to your mother and complaining that you're bored and unhappy. I have no idea how I managed to get roped into a caretaker role, but roped in I've been.'

'But I don't *want* you taking an interest in me!' she all but wailed. Luc, in passing, thought that was interesting because women usually wanted just the opposite out of him.

'I'm not taking an interest in you,' he disputed flatly. 'I'm broadening your work parameters: more interesting projects. Less back-room stuff. So you can start thinking about the wardrobe issue. Front-of-house demands a more stringent dress code than sacks and old shoes.'

'Okay, I will.' Just to bring the horrifying conversation to an end.

'And call me a mug, but I'm giving you a lift back to your house because I want to find out about this date of yours, satisfy myself that you're not about to put your life at risk with some low-life drifter. The last thing I need is my mother showing up at my office like an avenging angel because you've managed to get yourself into trouble.'

If she could have burrowed a hole in the soft, cream leather of the car seat and escaped to another county, Agatha would have done so. Never had she felt so humiliated in her life before. In all the scenarios that had played in her head over the years, not one had involved Luc taking an interest in her because he had no option. Nor had she ever envisaged being told that she looked like a bag lady, which was what he had implied.

She should never have accepted this job. No good ever came of accepting hand outs, although she knew that if she voiced that opinion he would have the perfect come back. Hadn't his own mother accepted a hand out of sorts when she had moved in with her parents in their rambling vicarage? That, to her way of thinking, was different, as was the dispenser of the hand out. Luc Laughton was hardly a kindly, middle-aged man charmed at the thought of doing a favour for a neighbour in need. He was a predatory shark who would have no qualms about eating the recipient of his charity if he felt like it.

'I can take care of myself,' she opined, staring straight ahead. 'I'm not going to get myself into any trouble.'

'You obviously haven't breathed a word of this so-called date to your mother,' Luc guessed shrewdly. 'Which leads me to think that you might be ashamed of him. Am I right?'

'I haven't said anything to Mum because I've only just *met* him!'

He noticed that she hadn't tackled the issue of whether she was ashamed of the man. Was he married? If he were to guess the kind of guy she would go for, it wouldn't be a married man. Her life had been nothing if not sheltered. His distant memory was of a girl with almost no sense of style, certainly not the sort of style favoured by her peer group: short, tight skirts, skinny, tight jeans, dangly jewellery. No, if he had to take a stab in the dark, he would bet his last few bucks on a fellow garden-lover, someone who got worked up about eco issues and saving the planet.

But if that were the case wouldn't she have been on the phone in a heartbeat to tell all to Edith? Even if, as she said, he had only recently landed on the scene.

'Is he married? You can tell me, although don't expect

me to give you my blessing, because I strongly disapprove of anyone getting entangled with someone who's married.'

Agatha's head jerked round at the cool contempt in his voice. Who did he think he was, she wondered? A shining example of morality? Normally reduced to quaking jelly in his presence, she took a deep breath and said very quickly in a very high, tremulous voice, 'I don't think you have a right to disapprove of anything.'

For a few seconds she actually wondered if he had heard her because he didn't say a word. She found that she was holding her breath, which she expelled slowly when he finally answered, his voice icy cold. 'Come again?'

'I've been given the job of buying all your discards their parting presents,' Agatha admitted tightly. 'Flowers, jewellery, expensive holidays—what's so great about having a string of pointless relationships? How can you preach about married men when you think it's all right to string some poor woman along knowing that you have no intention of getting involved with her?

Luc cursed fluently under his breath, outraged that she dared bring her opinions to bear on his private life. Not that he was about to justify his behaviour.

'Since when is pleasure pointless?' was all he said, clamping down on the rising tide of his temper because for Agatha fun without commitment would be anathema. When he had launched himself into the City, climbing that first rung of the ladder which he knew would lead him to the top, he had had the misfortune to fancy himself in love with a woman who had turned from a softly spoken angel to a harpy the second the demands of work had begun to interfere with her daily need to be stroked. She had complained solidly and noisily about meetings that over ran, had dug her heels in and lashed out at trips abroad and had eventually started looking elsewhere for someone who could give her undivided attention.

It had been a salutary lesson. So leading women up a garden path was definitely not a route he was interested in taking. From the very start, they knew that commitment wasn't going to be on the agenda. He was honest to a fault which, he personally thought, was a virtue to be praised, for it was in short supply in most men.

Which brought him back to the issue of this mysterious guy about whom she was being so secretive.

'But perhaps you don't agree with me,' he drawled, flicking a sidelong glance in her direction. 'Or maybe I'm wrong. Maybe you've been bitten by the big-city bug and come to the conclusion that there's nothing pointless in having fun. Is that it? I notice you still haven't mentioned Stewart's marital status.'

'Of course he's not married! He happens to be a very nice person. In fact, he's taking me out to a very expensive restaurant in Knightsbridge—San Giovanni. Stewart says that it's famous. In fact, you've probably heard of it.'

At which point, Luc's ears pricked up. This was definitely *not* the kind of man he'd pictured and, yes, he certainly had heard of the restaurant in question. It was the frequent haunt of the rich and famous.

So what did Agatha have that would attract someone who could afford to take her there? He shot her a sidelong glance and frowned; it struck him that she did have something about her, a certain innocence that a wide-boy Londoner might find suitably challenging. He didn't like to entertain the notion but sweet, prim Agatha might just be seen as ripe for corruption.

Not an eco-warrior, not a married man...so just someone out to use her? Or was he reading the situation all wrong?

Curiosity, lamentably in short supply in his life, shifted

somewhere inside him. He had acted on the spur of the moment in offering her a lift home, and really he should be heading back to his office to put the finishing touches to reports that needed emailing sooner than yesterday. But, hell, work could wait for a little while. Hadn't he been entrusted with a mission, in a manner of speaking?

In the space of seconds, plans for the remainder of his evening were put on hold.

'I'll drive you to Knightsbridge. And before you say anything…' his sensuous mouth curved into a half smile '… there's no need to thank me.'

CHAPTER TWO

Luc settled down with a cup of coffee for the long haul. Never mind about running late; it was his experience with women that their ability to get changed in under an hour was practically zero. Agatha might not follow the normal pattern of the women he knew, but she was of the female species. Enough said.

He glanced around the poky room with an expression of distaste. He had nothing against bedsits, per se, but it was evident that, whoever the landlord was, he specialised in the art of ripping off the young and inexperienced. The walls showed promising signs of damp and the single radiator looked like something rescued from the ark. The large, old-fashioned sash window overlooking the busy pavements was reasonably attractive but the wood was peeling, and he knew that if he stood too close to it he would be in danger of frostbite from the cold air blowing through the gaps in the frame. He wondered whether he should get more details about the guy. It would take next to no effort to put the fear of God into him.

He was restlessly pacing the room, stopping to scowl with displeasure at the hundred and one little deficiencies in her living accommodation to which Agatha had grown accustomed over the months, when she emerged from her bedroom.

'I got ready as quickly as I could. You didn't have to wait here for me. I could easily have got the tube back into London.'

Luc spun round at the sound of her voice behind him, and for a few seconds he stood very still, his stunning eyes unreadable—which was a disappointment. Although she hated the situation she was in, and hated the fact that he now considered her a burden with which he had to deal, he *did* still happen to be in her bedsit and she *was* quite dressed up. For her.

'How do you think I look?' she asked nervously, stretching out her arms and trying in to suck in her stomach.

An only child adored by her parents who had given up on ever having children until she'd come along, Agatha was still keenly aware that her figure didn't fit the trend, despite all the reassurances she had had growing up. She wasn't tall enough or skinny enough or flat-chested enough ever to look fashionable. Nor was her blond hair poker-straight.

But, having been insulted about her clothes, she had made a special attempt to look as smart as she could for her date—and incidentally to prove to Luc that she wasn't the complete fashion disaster that he seemed to think she was.

'You've done something to your hair,' he commented neutrally. She had a figure. Hell, how had he managed to miss that? It was weirdly shocking to see her in figure-hugging clothes that made the most of what he now registered, with a stunned attention to detail, as a tiny waist and the sort of lush breasts that made teenage boys and grown men stop in their tracks. When had she grown up? When had she stopped being a gauche, awkward teenager who hovered in the background and become…? He had to look away because his body had been galvanised into a response that stunned him.

'Well, I left it loose. It's so curly and unmanageable that I tie it up for work.'

'And it's heart warming to see that you possess something other than a flowing skirt and baggy jumper. It bodes well for your new approach to dressing for the office, although you might want to have a serious re-think about the length of the skirt.' Slender legs encased in sheer, black tights staged an all-out battle with his self-control. He was in the grip of utter, stupefied surprise—unfamiliar territory for him.

'What's wrong with it?' She bent slightly to inspect the hem of her dress with a frown. 'It's no shorter than some of the skirts the other girls wear.' She sighed, knowing what he meant without him having to spell it out. Short and tight was only acceptable on stick insects. 'Anyway,' she added defensively, 'I wouldn't dream of wearing anything like this to work. In fact, it's the only dress I have. Well, the only—'

He was reaching for her coat, clamping down on a reaction that he deemed inappropriate, inexplicable and ridiculous, and she winced at her propensity for rambling. Her mother had always called her a chatterbox and they had all been convinced at the garden centre that her success with the difficult plants lay in her ability to talk to them about anything and everything. But Luc wasn't interested in anything she had to say. She shut her mouth abruptly, and stiffly allowed herself to be helped into her coat.

'The only *what*?'

'It doesn't matter. It wasn't very interesting, anyway. I was just going to say that I don't have an awful lot of dresses. There was never much need to wear them when I worked at the garden centre.'

'I do recall some green overalls,' he drawled.

'I've never seen you at the garden centre.' Embarrassed colour was spreading to her hairline, and she was really relieved that he was following her so that he couldn't see her face.

'You would have remembered seeing me? That garden centre was pretty big.'

'Of course I would have remembered seeing you—be-cause…because you would have been so out of *place* there. I guess you might have been with Danielle. You might have a fleet of gardeners at the big house, but she always gets involved choosing the flowers, and the herbs, of course, for that little herb garden at the back of the kitchen.'

'No idea what you're talking about. I noticed you walking back to your house one evening in some green overalls and workman boots.'

Agatha flushed and had a vivid picture of how she must have looked to him, hurrying home still in her overalls, her boots dirty, her hair a tangled mess. And then in his office—no longer in overalls or dungarees but still dressed down in her comfortable, baggy clothes, while every other woman wafted around in high-heeled pumps and dapper little black or grey suits with their hair neatly combed back, obeying orders not to wriggle out of their pins and clips by mid-morning.

'I don't suppose you know a lot of women who would wear overalls and boots,' she said weakly, stepping into his car and slamming the door behind her.

'Not one.' He turned to her as he switched on the engine and the low, powerful car roared into life. 'In fact, the women I know wouldn't be seen dead in anything like that.'

'I know.'

'Really?'

'Well, I've seen the kind of women you've gone out with over the years. Not that I've taken any real interest, you un-derstand, but when Danielle lived with us you often came to visit with one of your girlfriends; they all looked the same, so I'm guessing you like them with lots of make-up and designer clothes.'

'Is there a sting in the tail with that remark?' Luc looked at her wonderingly before easing his car out of its parking space to head back towards the centre.

'I don't know what you mean.'

'No,' he said shortly, still unnerved by the underhand trick his body had played on him back there. 'I don't suppose you do.'

'What do you mean, then?'

'I mean that honesty is all well and good, but in London it might pay to be a bit more streetwise.' No wonder Edith worried about her. 'For one thing, you're being ripped off by your landlord. How much are you paying for that dump?'

'It's not a dump!' But she told him, and her heart sank when he gave a bark of cynical laughter.

'The man must have seen you coming a mile off. Green round the ears, no clue as to what sort of questions to ask, waving a stash of money. So what does he do? Overcharge for a disgusting hole with erratic heating and not enough space to swing a cat. Fifteen minutes in that place and I could spot enough signs of damp and rot to get the whole house condemned.'

'It's more comfortable when the weather's warm.'

'I bet it is.' Luc's lips curled with derision. 'You don't have to spend your nights praying that the place will be warm when you wake up in the morning! It's a disgrace.'

'I suppose,' Agatha admitted on a sigh. 'But when I looked around, Mr Travis promised that he would put right loads of things. I keep asking him, but his mother's been taken into hospital and the poor man's hardly been around.'

At this Luc burst out laughing before glancing across at her with rampant disbelief at her gullibility. 'So Poor Mr Travis has a sick mother in hospital which means that he just can't find the time to make sure that the damp problem in the bedsit gets seen to—or the rotting window frames get fixed, or the rancid carpet gets taken up? I wonder how poor Mr Travis would feel if a letter from my lawyer landed on his desk tomorrow morning.'

'You wouldn't!'

'Oh, I would, believe me. The man's a crook who's decided to take advantage of you. I'm not a superstitious guy, but I'm beginning to think that my mother's phone call was the hand of fate, because another month in that place in the middle of January and *you* would have been the one occupying the hospital bed—with pneumonia! No wonder you wear ten layers of clothing when you come to work. You've probably become accustomed to that!'

'I don't wear ten layers of clothes when I come to work.' The words 'charity case' were swimming in her head, making her feel nauseous.

'You weren't equipped for life in London.' Luc steamrollered over her interruption. 'You grew up in a vicarage and spent your short working life in a garden centre watering plants. I can't say that I enjoy being anybody's caretaker, but I'm beginning to see why my mother wanted me to get involved.'

'That's the most horrible thing you could ever say to me.'

'Why?'

'Because…' Because, a little voice said nastily, she didn't want Luc Laughton to think of her as a hapless country bumpkin who needed looking after. She wanted him to think of her as a sexy young woman—or even just as a *woman*. Fat chance! He hadn't even noticed her outfit. At least in any way that could be interpreted as complimentary.

'Well? I'm not in the habit of doing good deeds, but

I'm willing to change my life rules for you. You should be flattered.'

'No one's ever flattered to think that they're too stupid to take care of themselves,' Agatha told him stiffly. Her eyes stung but she wasn't going to feel sorry for herself. She was going to remember that she was about to have dinner with a dishy, eligible man who would never have asked her out if he had thought that she was as pathetic as Luc made her out to be.

'I've always found that it pays to be realistic,' Luc responded bracingly. 'When my father died and I came home to that financial mess, I realised very quickly that I could do one of two things: I could sit around, get depressed and become bitter or I could just go out and begin to rebuild everything that was lost.'

'I find it hard to think of you getting depressed or feeling bitter.'

'I don't allow those negative feelings to influence what I do in life.'

'I wish I could be as strong minded as you,' Agatha was forced to concede, thinking of all the doubts she had nurtured over the years despite her very happy background.

When her friends had all started experimenting with make-up and going on diets so that they could look like the models in magazines, she had taken a back seat, knowing that inner beauty was all that mattered, and that wanting to look like someone else or aspire to someone else's life was a waste of time. Of course, in London, the whole inner-beauty conviction had taken a bit of a knocking. She had largely felt like a fish out of water when she had gone out with her girlfriends from work, who had developed amazing skills of transformation, morphing from office workers to vamps with a change of clothes and bold make-up. Her stretchy black dress which made her feel horrendously exposed because it was fairly short with a fairly revealing neckline was still conservative compared to the stuff some of her friends wore, and she was so unaccustomed to wearing jewellery that she had to stop herself from twiddling with the strands of chunky copper round her neck.

'I mean,' she continued, musing, 'You're so sure of yourself. You set your goals and you just go after them. Like a bloodhound.'

'Nice comparison,' Luc muttered under his breath.

'Don't you ever sit back and wonder if you're doing the right thing?'

'Never.' With more than half the journey completed, Luc thought that it was time he got down to the business of quizzing her about her date. More and more, he got the feeling that she was a loose cannon, an innocent released to the mercy of any passing opportunist. 'So this Stewart character…?' he prompted.

Brought back down to earth with a bump, Agatha blinked. Her mind had been wandering. She had almost forgotten about Stewart.

'Yes…?'

'How did you meet him?'

'Oh, usual way,' she said with a casual, studied shrug; this was the perfect opportunity to prove to him that she wasn't as abnormal as he seemed to think she was. 'At a bar. You know…'

'At a bar? You go *bar hopping*?'

'When you say "bar hopping"…'

'Moving from *bar* to *bar*,' Luc intoned very slowly, emphasising each word. 'Getting more and more drunk before finally landing up somewhere, barely able to stand.'

Agatha bid a fond farewell to nurturing that misconception for him. The whole idea sounded pretty disgusting. She had heard ample stories of girls who had got themselves in trouble by doing just that sort of thing. Her father had counselled at least three that she could remember.

'When you told me that you were worried about me getting into trouble, that's not what you were talking about, was it? You didn't really think that I might end up pregnant by some guy whose name I never found out because I had gone out and had too much to drink, did you?'

'Calm down. I don't think you're the kind of girl.'

Insult or compliment? she wondered. Compliment, she decided. 'I met him at a wine bar. Near the office, actually. I went there with a couple of girls from work. We were having a drink and the bar tender brought over a bottle of champagne and told us that Stewart had sent it for me. When I looked over, he waved and then he came across to join us, and he and I ended talking for quite a while.'

'What about?'

'Lots of things,' Agatha told him irritably. 'He's very interesting. And very smart. Also good-looking.'

'I'm beginning to get the picture.'

'He wanted to know all about what I did, which was great, because most guys just like talking about themselves.'

'I didn't realise that you were that experienced.'

'I'm not experienced…with men in London. Naturally I've been out with quite a few boys at home, and generally speaking they just want to talk about football or cars. Very stereotypical.' She slid her eyes across to Luc, and as usual her mouth suddenly went dry, and she felt hot and flustered for no apparent reason. This was the first real conversation she had ever had with him, and she was enjoying herself, much as she loathed to admit it. 'What do you talk about when you go out with a woman?' she found herself asking curiously.

'Strangely enough, I find that it's the women who tend to do all the talking.' He had little interest in holding hands over the dinner table and sharing his thoughts with someone he planned on bedding.

'Perhaps you make a good listener,' Agatha suggested doubtfully. 'Although I'm not really sure that you do. You didn't listen to me when I told you that I could take care of myself.'

'And evidence of your living conditions proves that I was right on that score.'

'Maybe I should have been a little more insistent with Mr Travis,' she conceded, giving a little ground on this one thing—because he had yet to discover, in addition to all the other problems he had listed, the temperamental fridge and its even more temperamental close relative, the oven. 'But I'm a big girl when it comes to dealing with everything else.'

'That's true enough on the surface,' Luc murmured. 'You might look the part but I have a feeling that it only runs skin deep.'

'Look the part?' Was he telling her that she was fat? She might not be a stick insect, but she wasn't fat—plump, maybe, but not fat. And, if that was what he had meant, why was she stupidly asking for confirmation? Did her capacity for masochism never end?

'You're a big girl, Agatha. Funny, I hadn't really noticed until now.' Again he tried to equate the teenager with the woman next to him, and again that weird kick that shot through his body as if he had been suddenly hot-wired.

'You mean the dress?' she suggested in a taut voice. The very same dress she had exhibited for him, hands outstretched, vainly hoping that he might compliment her. They had reached the restaurant, but she wasn't quite ready to drop the conversation, so when he parked and turned towards her she garnered her very small supply of courage and stayed put, arms folded, her full mouth flattened into a thin line. 'I'm not ready to go in just yet.'

'Pre-dinner nerves? Don't worry. If he's that good-looking, that charming and that interested in every word you have to say, I'm sure you're in for a scintillating evening.'

'It's not pre-dinner nerves. It's…it's *you!*'

'I have no idea what you're talking about.'

'You haven't said one nice thing to me all evening. I know you would never have employed me to work for your company. I know you've been forced to help me out because you think you owe my family a favour—which you don't, but you could at least *try* and be nice. You've told me that I'm no good at what I do…'

She tabulated all her points by sticking up her fingers one by one. 'You've told me that the clothes I wear to work are horrendous because I don't wear that uniform of tight suits and high heels, even though I'm hidden away most of the time. I need to invest in a new wardrobe just in case someone important sees me and falls into a dead faint, I suppose. You've told me that I wouldn't have a clue how to look after myself in a place like London, you've told me how awful my bedsit is, and now? Now you sit there telling me that I look *fat!*'

Listing all those slights out loud hadn't been a good idea. Taken one at a time, she could reason them away, but faced with all of them in their entirety was just too much. A wave of forlorn self-pity rushed over her; her eyes began to leak and it wasn't long before the leak became a flood. When she found a handkerchief pressed into her hands, she accepted it gratefully and dabbed her eyes as her silly crying jag was reduced to the odd hiccup.

Embarrassment replaced self-pity. She blew her nose and stuffed the hankie into her bag.

'Sorry. Sorry, sorry, sorry. I must be nervous; you're right.'

'I should be the one apologising.' Luc had no time for weeping, wailing women, but for some reason the sight of Agatha in floods of tears had struck right to the heart of him. Hearing her neat little summary of everything he had said to her over the course of the evening had not been one of his proudest moments.

'It's okay,' she whispered, desperate to remove herself from his presence where seconds before she had wanted to stay and speak her mind. She tilted her face to him. 'Do I look a mess? I bet my make-up's everywhere. What's he going to think?' She gave a wobbly laugh.

'That you've got amazing eyes and that you're anything but fat,' he said roughly.

And just like that the atmosphere altered with sudden, sizzling electricity. It was as if the world had suddenly shrunk to the small space between them. She thought she could actually hear the rush of blood through her veins but then she realised that she was just imagining it. Thinking straight, this was the man who hadn't had a good word to say to her.

'You don't have to say that.'

'No. I don't.' But his voice had changed imperceptibly. 'But, just for the record, you do have amazing eyes, and when I said that you're a big girl now I didn't mean it in the literal sense.'

'You didn't?'

'I meant you've grown up. That dress makes you look sexy.'

'Sexy? Me?'

'You. Why do you sound so shocked?'

Because you're saying it, she thought, while her face burnt and her pulses raced and her heart sang. 'Let's hope

Stewart agrees!' Just in case those laser-sharp eyes of his could bore a hole in her head and pluck out that inappropriate thought.

'Stewart. The hot date. Yes.' His voice was clipped and he reached to open his car door. 'I'll come in with you. Hang on...' He leaned across and carefully rubbed his finger under her eye, and then he laughed softly when she jerked back in surprise.

'Relax. Just a bit of smudged mascara. Anyone would think you'd never been touched before, Agatha.'

'I...I have my hankie. Well, *your* hankie. I can do that! Could you switch on the light? I need to have a look at my face. Make sure my eyes aren't too puffy.' She laughed shrilly, and then chattered and tutted and avoided eye contact as she inspected her face in her little hand mirror, so that by the time she had finished dabbing and rubbing she could present him with a bright, tinny smile.

'Right, all ready! Can't wait!'

Three and a half hours later, a driving, bitter rain greeted her outside.

'So, when can I see you again?'

Agatha looked at Stewart who was pressed a bit closer to her than she would have liked—unavoidable because they were both sheltering under his umbrella. She had made sure that the buttons on her coat were done up to the neck. Whilst it had been flattering to be the object of his compliments, she had felt uncomfortable under his roving eye, even though she knew that this was what she should have expected. Several times she had caught him addressing her cleavage.

Also, her mind had been all over the place, analyzing and re-analysing everything Luc had said to her, then picking apart what she remembered of their conversation so that she could begin the process all over again. She had had to ask Stewart to repeat himself several times, had failed to notice the quality of the wine, which he had brushed aside—although she knew that he had been offended from the mottled colour of his neck—and had left most of her main course because she had accidentally ordered the wrong thing from the menu, which was in Italian.

She had no idea why he wanted to see her for a second date, and it felt almost churlish to have to think about it when he had been so good to overlook her little lapses and show so much interest in everything she had to say about every aspect of her life and job, however insignificant the detail.

'Tomorrow's Saturday,' he murmured. 'I know a great little club in Chelsea. Anybody who's anybody is a member. You wouldn't believe the famous faces I've spotted there; you'd love it.'

'Maybe we can do something next week.'

Stewart pouted with disappointment but picked himself up with remarkable ease, and as he reached out to hail a cab he pulled her close to him and, before she could wriggle away, planted a hot, laughing kiss full on her mouth.

'Sure I can't tempt you back to my place? I make a pretty good Irish coffee, if I say so myself.'

Agatha laughed and declined, and was guiltily relieved when he slid into the taxi, taking his umbrella with him, cheerily insouciant to the fact that she was now in the process of being drenched. And would therefore have to hail a cab, even though a taxi ride back to North London would be a ridiculous waste of money.

And, now that she did require one, there were none to be spotted. Although...

A familiar silver car pulled up to the kerb and she found the passenger door pushed open, waiting for her to oblige.

'Get in, Agatha. Or risk pneumonia.'

'Wow. How did you do that—show up just when I was

about to start walking to the underground? Anyway...' she straightened '...I can't have you messing up your Friday night to give me a lift home because you feel sorry for me.' She dug her hands into her pockets and began walking towards the underground while the car trailed her, sped up and then the passenger door was flung open again and Luc was glaring out at her from the driver's seat.

'Get in or I'll have to get out, lift you up and chuck you in. Do you want that? Do you want that kind of scene in the middle of Knightsbridge?'

'Have you been here the whole time waiting for me?' she asked as soon as she was inside the car, luxuriating in the warmth and dryness.

'Don't be crazy, but I had to come back here for you.'

'Why on earth would you have to do that? I know you think I'm a hopeless case, but I've been getting to and from work every day on public transport. I know how to use the buses and tubes! Course, it took a little time, but I got there in the end. Mum hates it. She keeps telling me that tubes are a breeding ground for muggers. And she's only been to London a handful of times—and never on a tube! Gosh, sorry; I'm talking too much again.' But like a bad dream all thoughts of her date had disappeared like a puff of smoke.

'I got Antonio to call me when you were about to pay the bill.'

'Who's Antonio?'

'The owner of the place. We go back a long way.'

'What if Stewart and I had decided to move on to somewhere else—a club, or a bar? Or I could just have decided to go back to his place.'

'Did he ask you to?'

'As a matter of fact, he did.'

'And you turned him down. Good girl. Wise decision.'

'Who knows what I'll say the next time he asks, though?'

She looked across at him. He had changed out of his work clothes into a pair of dark jeans and a thick, black jumper. His coat had been tossed to the back seat. She was ashamed to admit even to herself that if she had all the time in the world, she would never tire looking at him.

He opened his mouth as though on the verge of saying something, only to think better of it.

'So you've arranged another date, have you?'

'Not as such...' She teased those three little words out as long as she could. 'Who knows?'

'Who knows indeed?' Luc intoned in a peculiar voice.

'What have you done this evening?' she asked a little breathlessly.

'Work. I've been working on, eh, a very interesting project, let's just say.'

'Do you know, it's great that you enjoy your job so much,' Agatha said warmly. 'Although it's a little sad that you want to spend your Friday nights doing it.'

'Your honesty is beyond belief, Agatha. I would have entertained myself in the usual way, but there was something a little more important I had to do. After doing that, I realised that I needed to have a little chat with you. Let's just say that one thing gave rise to the other.'

'Why are you being mysterious? What do we need to chat about?' Why did the words 'little chat' inspire such feelings of dread? Was he about to sack her? Had she overstepped the line with her beyond-belief honesty?

Agatha quailed at the thought of returning to Yorkshire as a failed charity case—but London, even a bedsit in London, was impossible without a pay packet at the end of the month.

'This isn't the right place. I am going to take you to your house, you are going to ask me in for a cup of coffee and we can have our chat then.'

'Can't it wait until Monday?'

'I think it's better to get it out of the way. Now, relax; tell me about your evening. Take me through how a guy who leaves a woman standing in the pouring rain sees fit to entertain her.'

Now out of a job, Agatha didn't think she had anything to lose by being totally, one-hundred percent honest. People were never honest with Luc, with the exception of his mother. They tiptoed around him, bowing and scraping, 'yes, sir', 'no sir'. He was one of those lethally good-looking men who were just too powerful for their own good. He was unapologetic in his arrogance and in his assumption that he could play by his own unique set of rules.

'I don't want to be having this conversation with you.'

'Why not? Are you embarrassed? There's nothing to be ashamed of because it was a flop. These things happen. You just have to shrug it off and move on.' Furthermore, she would be glad of his sterling advice when he filled her in on a few missing jigsaw pieces. His Friday night had been ruined, but he was upbeat about it.

Without the hassle of traffic, it took them less than half an hour before he pulled up outside her house, and Agatha hadn't said a word for the brief drive. Her evening out had been disappointing, but there was a slow resentment building inside her at the way Luc had showed up for her, like a parent collecting a child from a birthday party. And then to hear him dismiss her date as a flop, something unfortunate that she should step over and forget with a shrug, made her even more angry.

She hadn't asked him to start interfering in her life. He had barely noticed her for the past eight months, but now that he had been forced to he had decided to give the project his full and complete attention. But he still couldn't conceal the fact that he found her annoying and a nuisance. Everything about her offended him, starting with the way she didn't seem to know how to suck up to him sufficiently, and ending with the way she looked—and Luc, being Luc, he made no bones about hiding his reaction.

And now he needed to chat to her. It could only be about her job. He had gone away, added up all the reasons why she didn't belong in his company and was going to break it to her that, however indebted he felt to her mother, having her as dead weight in his office was too steep a price to pay.

'I know what you're going to say,' she burst out as soon as he had killed the engine. 'And you can just tell me right here.' She had unclasped her seat belt, and now she swivelled round to look at him.

'You know what I'm going to say?'

'Yes. I know what you think of me, and I know exactly what you're going to say.' The words tumbled out with feverish urgency.

'I don't think you have a clue what I think of you,' Luc informed her huskily. 'And you certainly don't know what I'm going to say to you. And, no, we are not going to have this conversation in my car.'

'I just want to get it over and done with,' Agatha implored, but he was already out the car and she hurriedly followed suit, fumbling in her bag for the house key and feeling the tension escalate with every step up to her bedsit.

Stepping back into the room, she switched on the light and looked around it with new eyes, Luc's eyes. She took in the discoloured walls, which she had tried to hide by sticking up two large, colourful posters, the sagging, tired furniture, the stained carpet peeping out from behind the thin Moroccan rug she had put over it and the seeping cold. He was right; who else would put up with all that?

'I'm a failure, and you've come to terms with that, and you want to find a polite way of telling me to get lost,' she said in a rush, before she had even removed her coat. 'I'm sacked, aren't I?'

'Sacked? Why would I want to sack you?' Eyes as green as the deep ocean stared steadily at her. 'I want to tell you that I know Stewart Dexter and I know what he wants from you.'

CHAPTER THREE

'You know Stewart?' Agatha's mouth fell open and she gaped at him in complete bewilderment. 'I don't understand. You've never met him before; I didn't introduce you...'

'Take your coat off and sit down.'

'If you knew him, why didn't you come across to say hello?' While she hovered, frantically trying to unravel this unforeseen turn of events, she found herself being helped out of her coat. 'Well, I guess it's a good thing that I'm not being sacked,' she breathed shakily, clutching the one thing he had said that had made sense.

His fabulous green eyes settled on her and suddenly she felt very exposed in her tight black dress and her silly, high black shoes. It was a relief to sink into the chair facing him. When she glanced down, she was accosted by the embarrassing sight of her deep cleavage and abundant breasts straining against the soft, elastic fabric of her dress. She resolved to shelve the outfit first thing in the morning.

'But I don't understand why it was so important for you to race over to the restaurant to tell me this.'

'When you mentioned the name of the guy you were meeting, it rang a bell, but I didn't think anything of it,' Luc said carefully. 'I have a finger in a lot of pies and so I meet people from a range of industries. And Dexter is a common enough surname. But then I saw the guy at the restaurant and the alarm bells started ringing.'

'Alarm bells? I don't know what you're talking about.'

'You're not going to like what I have to say.' Never one to waste time beating about the bush, Luc now paused and considered his words carefully. Staring across the table at him, her eyes wide and perplexed, Agatha looked very, very young, and strangely enough the revealing nature of her dress only accentuated that impression.

'How old are you?' he asked roughly, finding himself momentarily sidetracked.

'Sorry?'

'Forget that. It's not important. There's no easy way to say this, but Dexter might not be the guy you think he is.'

'I really don't know what you're talking about. You mean Stewart Dexter *isn't* Stewart Dexter? Who is he, then?'

'He's someone who used to work for one my companies. When I thought I recognised him, I went back to the office and did a little research.'

'You ran a background check on my date?' Agatha trembled. 'How could you *do* that?' Her huge blue eyes, staring up at him, were full of reproach.

'I'd advise any woman to run a background check on a man they'd picked up in a bar before they went out with him on a date, Agatha. This isn't a small village in Yorkshire.'

'I'm not ashamed that I trust people, Luc. I know *you* don't, and I can understand why. Your father trusted George Satz and in return he had all his money stolen from him.'

The story had run in the local newspaper for weeks, with each new revelation of embezzlement producing a fresh torrent of speculation. With Elliot Laughton no longer around to defend himself, details went uncontested. Members of staff were interviewed and their bafflement at the scale of the financial losses only added to the scandal. At the time,

Agatha had felt deeply sorry for Luc, although that was something she would never have shared with him. He had returned from university with a protective barrier around him that repelled words of sympathy. The whole business would surely have accounted for the man he was later to become—a man who would never know how to give anyone else the benefit of the doubt.

Her meandering mind returned to the present and she cleared her throat. 'Well, almost all his money. So I can see why you're so suspicious of other people—but I'm not. It would never occur to me to do a background check on anyone! Anyway, we were meeting in a public place, and there was no way that I was going to go anywhere afterwards with him.' Her angry eyes locked with his and she leaned forward, her hands balled into fists.

'Like I told you,' Luc's voice was cool and even and controlled, 'You're not savvy about the kind of guy a girl can get mixed up with in London. Dexter was sacked from the company a year and a half ago. He was a minor cog in one of the IT companies I took over. He was caught trying to hack into confidential programs to do with software. He was kicked out the second the breach was discovered by one of my people.'

'I don't believe you.'

'You don't *want* to believe me. And I don't *want* to be sitting here telling you this. But some good Samaritan's got to fill you in on the man. Naturally, in the case of a dismissal of that nature, no references were forthcoming. He disappeared and, as far as I know, he isn't working for any of the major players in the country. Did he mention the name of his employer?'

'No.' Agatha was beginning to feel giddy. 'Are you sure about all this? I mean, it's easy to confuse people…to think you recognise someone when you don't know them really…'

'I don't make those kinds of mistakes.'

Agatha was immediately silenced.

'Everyone makes mistakes,' she muttered eventually.

Luc ignored that. 'I could find out what outfit Dexter managed to inveigle his way into and get him fired, not least because he would have had to forge his references from my company.'

'I'm not a child! If Stewart is really the person you think he is, then I can just ask him outright.'

'And I'm sure he would come up with a very convincing story.'

'And I would be so easy to convince, wouldn't I? Because I'm green round the ears.'

'How is it that you are so good at making me feel like a monster?' he murmured softly. An unnatural urge to put his arms around her was squashed before it could take form. 'I'm actually doing you a favour by telling you this.'

'It doesn't feel like a favour. Even if Stewart is who you say he is—and I'm still not certain that you haven't got it wrong; people do get things wrong, even people like you— well, what does that have to do with *me*?'

'I think Dexter sought you out.'

'Sought me out? That sounds like a bit of a conspiracy theory.' Agatha's head was in a whirl.

'Course, it all could be pure coincidence, but my gut feel is that he decided to set up in competition. Have you any idea of the value of gaming software? Which is why it's one of the most highly confidential areas of all my companies. I have computer-game designers working to create games that could outrun some of the biggest sellers. After Dexter's hacking attempts, I made sure that all entries were closed down. If he really wanted to get his hands on some of my developing ideas, he might have thought that he needed to go down a different route.'

Realisation was beginning to dawn for Agatha. Naturally, Luc could be off target with his assumptions, but would he really ever make a mistake like that? When it came to business, his acumen was legendary. Everyone in the company reverently believed that everything he touched turned to gold; only someone blessed with an ability to make sound decisions would ever have possessed that Midas touch.

'Question: has Dexter been asking you all sorts of questions about the company?'

Agatha twisted in her chair so that she could look at him. 'Of course he's been interested in what I have to say.'

'I'll bet.'

If only there had been a part of her that could really and truly believe that she hadn't been used, she would have run with it. Instead, all she could volunteer feebly, was, 'Everyone deserves a second chance. Even people who come out of prison get second chances.'

She belatedly realised how often the subject of her work had cropped up in the conversation. She had been flattered at the interest and had downplayed her role in the company. In fact, she hadn't mentioned the broom cupboard once.

'I think Dexter is manipulating you to access information,' Luc told her bluntly.

'What sort of information? This is too much. My head's beginning to spin.'

Feeling disadvantaged on the chair, Agatha stood up and weaved a wobbly path to the kitchen so that she could pour herself a glass of water. She returned to find Luc standing by the window and idly peering out. He turned when he heard her but remained where he was, six foot two of towering alpha male with the subtlety of a sledge hammer.

Suddenly she was really angry that Luc was the one who

had taken it upon himself to point her in the right direction by humiliating her and then calling it doing her a favour.

She realised how much she preferred the comfort of lusting from afar. Having her heart flutter whenever she glimpsed him at a distance had been a little inconvenient but it had never threatened her peace of mind. She could remember sitting in the snug at the vicarage, curled up with a book, half-reading it, half-pleasantly day dreaming about Luc suddenly noticing her and sweeping her off her feet. At seventeen, it had been a very nice day-dream.

A living, fire-breathing Luc with a mission to save her from herself was more than she could bear. He was just *too much*. She felt like a moth helplessly drawn to the blinding brightness of a fire, knowing that the nearer she got the more dangerous her situation became.

She didn't want him to turn his attention to her; she didn't want him to think that he had to look after her because she was incapable of looking after herself. She wanted him back at arm's length and she knew that, if she could only put him there, then she would be able to get on with her life.

Agatha blinked and snapped back to the present. 'You were saying… Um, you were going to tell me what information you think Stewart wants to drag out of me. I don't know anything about computer software. I have a laptop in my bedroom, but I hardly ever use it. When I do, it's just to email.'

Luc looked at her flushed face: her half-parted mouth, her wide, incredulous eyes and that cloud of tousled fair hair that made her resemble a naughty, slightly dishevelled angel. A very sexy angel. He found that it was a struggle not to let his eyes dip to the generous curve of her breasts.

He pushed himself away from the window, suddenly restless, but it was a very small room. From whatever angle, he seemed to be confronted with the sight of her smooth skin, the shadow of her cleavage, the slope of her shoulders and her hair tumbling over them.

'You're mistaken if you think that Stewart has hunted me down so that he could use me to pick my brain about your state secrets.'

'*You* know that you wouldn't recognise one of those state secrets if it lay down in front of you waving a white flag and begging to be discovered. And I know that. But *he* doesn't, does he?'

'Oh, this is hopeless.' She had been so optimistic that life as a single girl in the dating game would begin with Stewart. But the date had failed to live up to its promise, and now this.

'The man is using you, and you have to get rid of him. Never mind the personal angle. From my point of view, you become a liability the minute your trustworthiness is in question.' He had tough lines on company security. There were no loops through which anyone could wriggle.

Agatha gaped at him. 'Even though you *know* that I would never do anything? Even though I've just told you how hope-less I am when it comes to understanding all that computer jargon? Are you saying that you don't *trust* me?'

Luc shrugged and lowered his eyes. 'Sex and pillow talk can work the strangest magic. Who's to say that he wouldn't talk you into a little hanky panky at the office when every-one else has left for the evening? He knows the layout of the building. There's virtually no chance that he could hack into anything important but I'm not willing to risk a situation that could cost me millions.'

Agatha wasn't even sure that she would have continued seeing Stewart. She had felt no real connection there. But this was about principles.

'I'll...I'll think about what you said.'

'You'll have to do a bit more than that, I'm afraid.'

'Or else I'm out of a job?'

'Regrettably.'

Agatha didn't think that he looked like a man wracked with remorse at the situation—but then dispatching a charity case wouldn't exactly bring him out in a bout of cold sweat and panic, would it? She was utterly disposable. Always one to see the silver lining in the cloud, she slumped into the chair, battered and dismayed.

Luc steeled himself and let the silence stretch between them, then he left quietly, shutting the door with a click that resonated in the room like a time bomb.

Having dug deep and uncovered Dexter for the manipulative and possibly dangerous charmer that he was, Luc had expected a positive response from Agatha. If, for instance, someone had offered him concrete proof that a woman he was dating was in it solely for the money, he knew that he would be only too quick to shed the offending gold-digger. But, then again, he was a realist through and through. Agatha was not; he had to face it.

Instead of falling on his neck with relief that he had spared her the misery of dating a guy who wanted to use her, she had been disbelieving, argumentative and had eventually put him in the position of having to issue her with an ultimatum.

What was it they said about no good deed going unpunished?

Famed for an ability to jettison pointless aggravation, Luc found himself spending the weekend in an unsettled frame of mind. He couldn't believe that she would choose a man she barely knew over his impeccable advice, not to mention over a job that was extravagantly well paid for what it was. And the prospect of firing her—whilst he would have no option if she didn't dump Dexter—wasn't something that filled him with enthusiasm. His mother had rarely asked anything of him; she was stoic by nature. Even when she had found herself at the mercy of the unforeseen, when the full story of the company collapse had emerged, she had not once looked to him for the solution; her only instinct had been to protect him from the cruelty of the press. So the thought of letting her down now was not a pleasant one.

By six on Sunday evening he was primed to do the unthinkable and he didn't waste time debating the pros and cons.

The conference call he had scheduled was cancelled with the minimum of excuses, and by seven Luc was parked outside Agatha's house in his Aston Martin. Looking up to her floor, he could see that it was in darkness. Having rung the doorbell twice to no avail, and telephoned her landline three times, he was confident that she wasn't in. He would wait—no big deal.

He didn't stop to analyse the wisdom of showing up at her bedsit to find out whether she had made her decision: Dexter or the job.

The foul humour that had been his constant companion over the weekend was dissipating. He almost missed her dark outline as she scurried towards the front door of the converted Victorian house, fumbling in her bag and dropping the key twice in the process.

Nor was Agatha aware of his car sandwiched innocuously along the kerb between a motorbike and a small white van. Frankly, she wasn't aware of very much as she scrabbled with shaking fingers to get the key in the door.

Her head was buzzing. She was utterly oblivious to the sound of his footsteps as he vaulted out of his car towards her, surprising her just as she had managed to turn the key and was opening the front door.

Agatha reacted with a shriek and, her nerves already in

shreds, swung her right arm at her assailant propelled by the full weight of her voluminous bag. The blow caught him a cracking direct hit on the side of his face.

'Good God, woman!'

Agatha squinted in the dark and recognised Luc as he nursed his jaw. Uncharacteristically, she was sorely tempted to hit him again, but instead she walked quickly into the dark hall and attempted to slam the door in his face.

Having waited for over an hour in his car for her to return, there was no way that Luc was having that. Indeed, having a woman slam a door in his face, whatever the reason, was not on his list of acceptable behaviour. He elbowed his way in, still nursing his jaw, so that she was forced to look at him.

'What are you doing here?'

'Right at this very moment in time? Wondering whether you've broken anything.'

'You shouldn't creep up on people and then you won't get hit.'

'I'm beginning to think that looks can be deceiving with you.' He lowered his hand, having satisfied himself that there was no need to visit the casualty department of the local hospital just yet.

'I don't want to talk to you.'

'Why not? Where have you been?'

'None of your business. Go away.'

'You know I'm not going to do that. We never reached a conclusion after our last conversation.'

He kept pace with her easily as she climbed the two flights to her bedsit, and before she could get any ideas about locking him out he insinuated himself into the front room behind her and then leaned against the door, watching her.

'I told you I don't want to talk to you,' Agatha muttered,

although she didn't know why she bothered to waste her breath because here he was, larger than life, in her room, waiting to get his wretched answer. It was no longer just a case of her being a ninny and getting involved with an undesirable guy, but a case of it affecting part of his company. She could understand his anxiety, but that didn't mean that she liked him being here again, making her feel awkward and self-conscious.

She got rid of her coat. Luc noted that the sexy outfit of the day before had been replaced by her stock-in-trade long skirt, thick tights just visible above her sensible black lace-ups and what looked like layers of cloth, culminating in a grey cardigan which she had buttoned to the neck. And then from nowhere he was knocked for six by a graphic image of her back in that dress, then stepping out of it wearing nothing underneath, naked, warm and pliant, leaning back so that he could play with her abundant breasts, splay his fingers against her thighs, lead her hand to his erection...The immediate stirring in his loins shocked him and he turned away abruptly and forced himself to think straight.

'I know.'

Agatha glared and shifted her weight from foot to foot, feeling his presence in the room like a suffocating weight.

'He's not worth it, you know,' Luc said harshly. The lights from the street filtered up, turning her hair to silver as it brushed in curls along her jawbone and down to her shoulders. He wondered how he had never noticed the delicacy of her features—wide eyes, a small, straight nose, a full mouth and a heart-shaped face. Maybe it was because she made it her duty never to look him fully in the eye if she could help it.

'How did you know that I went to see him?' she asked now, conforming to his theory of avoidance by staring down at the rug. 'Well, it doesn't matter. It's finished. So you don't have to worry about him enticing me into a compromising situation.'

'That's…a good outcome,' Luc said dismissively, eyes narrowed—and now she did look at him, her cheeks flushed with anger.

'I really *hate* you!' she burst out, tears forming in the corners of her eyes. 'You don't care about anyone's feelings, do you? The only thing you care about is your stupid company! You don't care that Stewart is…*was*…the first date I'd had since I moved to London!'

'And what a date he turned out to be. If you think your heart's breaking now, try projecting yourself down the road six months from now if you'd carried on going out with him! How do you think it would have felt when he turned around and dumped you because you couldn't give him what he wanted? Or when he found out that you didn't have access to the IT part of my company?'

'How can you be so *cold*?' The worst of it was that he was right. The minute she had lied to Stewart and said that she'd decided to hand in her notice—just a little white lie with her fingers crossed behind her back—she had felt him backing away from her faster than a speeding train. They had met at a small restaurant halfway between the city and her house, and his enthusiasm for the bill when she had started waxing lyrical about the stresses of working for a big company and her need to get back to a job close to nature would have been funny if she hadn't been so disillusioned. She would never know if he had wanted to get to those company secrets, as Luc had suggested, but she had to think that he really had used her to find a way into the company even if only to cause mischief for Luc having sacked him.

She knew that he was shallow and manipulative, and probably had a raging temper, which she had glimpsed for one frightening moment, but that still didn't do her ego much good.

And Luc, standing there and sneering, felt like the final straw.

'You don't know what it's like to…to think that something's going somewhere and it turns out that you've been completely wrong!' she yelled. 'You're like a block of ice!'

'He was a creep.'

'Yes, I *know* he was a creep! You don't have to tell me that. And I know I wouldn't have ended up having a relationship with him, but it would have been nice if I hadn't had my nose rubbed in it!' She stood up, shaking like a leaf, and walked towards him. 'It's easy for you because you don't *want* to get involved with anyone!'

'I did you an enormous favour.'

'Well, I don't feel much like thanking you for it.'

They were only inches apart now. Agatha didn't quite know how her feet had taken her towards him, and up this close she because dizzily aware of the golden flecks in his irises. All of a sudden it was as though the air had been knocked out of her body. He was staring down at her, his dark face perfectly still.

'Feel better?' he asked softly and she blinked, mesmerised by his voice. 'You needed to get angry, Agatha.'

'I…I don't get angry.' The gentleness in his voice sent her into a confusing, giddy tailspin. Her face felt hot and her heart was hammering in her chest so that she could barely manage to get her breath out.

'If you don't get angry now and again, you'll find that people will walk all over you. Say the word, and I would be more than happy to get angry with that loser on your behalf.'

Agatha blinked. That felt like the nicest thing that had

ever been said to her, but she didn't understand why because she was so angry with him: *wasn't she?*

'I don't believe in violence.'

'Sit. I'll get you a coffee.'

'Are you being nice to me?'

His mouth softened into a ghost of a smile which made her toes curl. She sat down, trying to gather herself while she listened to the sounds of him in the kitchen, opening and shutting cupboards and clumsily trying to make her something hot to drink. She had taken a real bruising earlier on and the prospect of being on her own with just her thoughts for company made her go cold inside.

Besides, this was a side to him that she hadn't seen before, and it was the side she suspected had the women flocking to him in droves. Because, rich or poor, Luc would always have had his fan club lining up to do whatever he wanted. When he squatted at her feet, depositing the mug on the little table he pulled towards her, she felt special. It was ridiculous, and she wanted to fight the feeling, but her encounter with Stewart had weakened all her defences.

'You were right, anyway. I don't belong here in London.'

'Because you got taken in?' He sat next to her and angled his long body so that he was facing her, his hands lightly clasped on his thighs.

'Because I wasn't sharp enough or streetwise enough to spot him.' Luc was so close to her that their arms were nearly touching. When he reached out and caught her fluttering fingers in his hand, she jumped and moved to tug her hand away but then thought better of it. It was a gesture of consolation. She was miserable. It was the first time he had ever touched her in a deliberate way, and her body responded with a surge of heated awareness that made her feel faint.

'Anyway.' She struggled to get her thoughts in order.

She still couldn't bring herself to look at him for fear that the dual onslaught of those fabulous, sexy eyes and the feel of his long fingers playing with hers would make her do something really, really stupid—especially given the fragile state of mind she was in. So instead she breathed in deeply and gulped.

'It's no good me working for you; I think you'll agree with me. I know you were made to help me out, and I'm very grateful, but I'm a liability—you said so yourself. What if you hadn't recognised Stewart? What if he had…done whatever it was you thought he would do? It's not as though I would have clued up and smelled a rat.'

She gave a choked, hysterical laugh. 'I have no experience of big business, or of finance. Or of anything, for that matter.' She thought back to her high hopes when she had first arrived in London. She had counted all the positives of stepping outside her comfort zone. She had recognised that small-village life might have been fine as a kid but that there wasn't a single young woman she knew who wouldn't trade it for the experience of working in a top company in London. She had thought she would throw herself into office life and gain lots of invaluable experience. She would make dozens of new, exciting friends and into that heady mix would come lots of boyfriends.

Yes, she had made lots of friends, but her optimism about forging a career in an office had proved to be ill-founded. She'd struggled with her computer course and she had become the dumping ground for work no one else wanted to do. How one earth could she hope to compete with all those bright young things with their degrees in economics and languages?

And where were all those thrilling young men who were going to rush in to replace her hopeless crush on Luc Laughton? Few and far between.

'I feel much better now,' she said in an unnaturally high voice and she offered him a watery smile. 'I'm definitely not going to get angry again.'

'Why not? I'm tough. I can take it.'

'I'm going to be realistic,' she told him, while her heart continued to beat a steady, crazy drum roll inside her. 'I'm going to cut my losses and go back to Yorkshire. There's no point in looking for another office job in London, and I've been to Kew Gardens to ask them if there were any vacancies and there were none. I've been thinking of doing a landscaping course. I'd like that. I'm not cut out for anything else.'

'Why don't you look at me when you're talking to me? I don't bite.'

He had kept his voice low and amused, but her refusal to meet his gaze was really beginning to get on his nerves. Was she so terrified of him or was she scared witless that something might show in her eyes—resentment at being put in the unenviable position of supplicant, manoeuvred there against her will?

He hadn't been kidding when he had told her that looks could be deceptive when it came to her, and that flash of anger which he had provoked had hinted at a passionate nature lurking below the surface. Was it something that she was aware of and shied away from?

Agatha looked up into those glittering, unreadable eyes and fought for something sensible to say, but her mouth was dry and all she could see in her mind's eye was his beautiful face close to hers, and all she could hear was her racing heartbeat and the rush of blood in her ears.

'So this is what you've been hiding.' He had never suspected it. She had managed to maintain such a low profile that even his highly developed antennae had missed it.

'What?' Agatha managed to squeak in a preternaturally high voice.

The silence thrummed between them. Agatha found that she could hardly breathe as he continued to stare at her, his dark, winged eyebrows raised speculatively.

'Is it because I've caught you in a vulnerable moment?'

'I don't know what you're talking about.'

'Course you do,' he chided softly, reaching out to brush one long finger against her cheek—then finding his body charged with a savage, urgent want that descended so fast and so hard that he sucked his breath in sharply. Agatha shuddered and closed her eyes and rested against the back of the sofa, her body yearning up towards him.

With a stifled groan, he pulled her towards him with a hungry, impatient urgency. Her hair was like silk as he curled his fingers into its tousled length.

Agatha stepped from fantasy to reality and was lost. This moment had been the fodder for a thousand dreams—a *million* dreams! A rush of heady, surreal intensity raced through her body with cyclonic force and she felt a wetness between her legs that made her want to rub her thighs together restlessly. Was this really happening? His mouth on hers was explosive, and she surrendered to it with a whimper of pleasure, her hands pulling him towards her and her body moulding against his as they fell back on the sofa.

Always in control of any situation with a woman, Luc found himself in the novel place of losing all control.

'You're not in a good place at the moment,' he murmured, striving to insert some rationality.

'Don't talk. Please don't talk. I…I want it. I want you.' She exulted in the feel of his muscled body as she shamelessly weaved her hands under his shirt and ran her fingers along the hard planes of his chest. The fantasy had been gentle and dreamlike. The reality was ferocious, dramatic and mind-blowing. Her body had parted company with her brain and common sense was being dragged along in the wake of a surging need that had swelled to an irresistible force in the space of seconds.

He shifted against her and the feel of his erection pushing hard against her stomach brought a responding need pooling like honey inside her.

'Let's go to the bedroom,' she half-moaned, half-pleaded.

If there was a fractional hesitation, Agatha didn't see it. Her eyes were half-closed and her body was in meltdown. She groaned feverishly when he eased himself off the sofa, taking her with him and laughing softly under his breath when she told him that she was too heavy to be lifted.

'How weak do you think I am?' he asked hoarsely, settling her on the bed, and then standing to appreciate the sight of her rumpled sexiness. But not for long. He couldn't shed his clothes fast enough, and he couldn't get enough of the way she was watching him, her eyes shy and greedy at the same time. It was the biggest turn-on he had ever had.

A shard of common sense prompted him to ask, 'Are you sure about this?'

Her nod was the only encouragement he needed.

CHAPTER FOUR

Luc looked appreciatively at the woman lying on the bed in front of him—warm, willing and wide-eyed. The force of his craving slammed into him with the unstoppable power of a runaway train. He seriously couldn't remember the last time a woman had provoked an urgent response like this. Was it true that variety was the spice of life? Had he become too accustomed to that Western view of beauty which dictated that it came only in a long, thin package? He didn't know and he didn't stop to analyse his body's unusual response.

His natural instinct took over and he shed the remainder of his clothes, making sure to take his time, to pace himself, enjoying her absorption in the details of his nudity.

When he sank onto the bed next to her, she trembled and released a soft, yearning sigh.

'You're beautiful,' Luc imparted in a voice that was rich, deep and unbearably erotic.

'That's not what you said before.'

'Your clothes don't do you justice.'

'I'm not thin enough,' Agatha felt compelled to point out, heady and exultant to be living a dream she had always considered out of reach, and he groaned in response as he gently began to ease her out of her top.

'I'm beginning to think that thinness is a much-overrated virtue,' he growled huskily as he feathered a finger along the inside of her bra strap, curving it along the soft fullness of her breast and watching in fascination as her nipple tightened under the lace.

Without completing the manoeuvre of taking off the bra, he instead chose to flick his tongue against her nipple as it struggled to peep out from between the swirls of lace. She writhed against him and he had to dig deep into his reserves of self-control not to take her right then, like a randy teenager having his first taste of sex.

Her breasts were big, bigger than he had always been led to assume from the nondescript, baggy clothing she had worn around the office. He liked it. A lot. In fact, it was driving him crazy.

Taking his time was all well and good in theory but practice was proving nigh-on impossible.

An expert when it came to undressing a woman, he found that he couldn't get to grips with the niggly clasp of the bra and would have happily ripped it off had she not reached behind her, with her eyes still closed, to unhook it from behind.

'I must be losing my touch…'

He was barely aware of her breathlessly telling him that his touch felt just perfect to her. He was way too absorbed in the sight of her breasts as they spilled out of their delicate restraints.

The big, pink discs of her nipples with their erect buds standing to attention pouted up at him, begging for his mouth.

Who was he to deny them both the pleasure?

He cupped them in his big hands and massaged them, rolling his thumbs over the stiffened crests before bending so that he could devote one-hundred percent of his undiluted attention to driving her crazy.

As he licked and suckled, first one, then the other, he wasn't completely sure who was being pleasured more.

When he pushed his hand below the waistband of her jeans, she literally gasped and shuddered in wild anticipation.

'Please...' Agatha curled her fingers into his hair and looked down to where his dark head was roving over her breasts, tasting them and teasing them, and drawing her nipple into his mouth so that he could savour them even more.

'Please...what?'

'I...I want you.' Her voice broke on an admission that would have been inconceivable only hours ago.

'How much?' Since when had he ever asked that question of any woman?

Agatha's eyes flickered open and she gazed at him raptly, then she gave a nervous little laugh. 'I know this is mad but I want you so much.' She ran her hand along the length of his torso, marvelling at this new-found wantonness he seemed to have brought out in her. Where had that come from? Her just uttering those words was shocking and thrilling at the same time. 'And I don't want to talk.'

'Sometimes talking can be sexy...'

Which she discovered, as he talked *and* touched, commenting on her body, as he began to unzip her jeans, telling her what he would like to do to it.

It was very, very sexy. She couldn't wait to get out of her jeans. They felt like glue against her body and as he began to tug them down she helped him, kicking them off and sending them flying to join the rest of her clothes that were heaven only knew where on the ground.

'How wet are you for me?' Luc breathed into her ear, stopping to watch her face with a crooked smile on his.

'You're embarrassing me!' She barely recognised herself.

'You're enjoying it. I like that. I never suspected…But then when you looked at me…' He circled her nipple with his fingers, zeroing in on the taut bud and playing with it till she was panting and moaning. 'Well? How much do you want this?' he pressed her softly with amusement, half at her languorous, feline movements, half at himself because he wasn't usually this vocal or, for that matter, so uncool.

'More than you know.'

The effect of those few words on him was electrifying. Discarding her underwear, he slid two fingers into her, stroking her on that most sensitive of spots so that she wriggled against his hand, pushing and arching, and dimly hoping that the walls weren't as thin as she suspected they might very well be.

'Oh no you don't,' he laughed softly; he removed his hand and began working his way down the flat planes of her stomach with his mouth.

Agatha's eyes flew open and she gave a protesting squeak.

'You can't!'

Luc interrupted his ministrations to shoot her a quizzical look from under his lashes then he gave her a devastating smile and positioned himself squarely between her legs.

Still looking at her, imagining the rosy blush invading her cheeks—because it was dark enough in the room to hide all but her most obvious reactions—he brought his mouth down to nuzzle against her damp mound.

Her instinct was to buck against him but he held her down and, lord, that questing mouth, exploring her most intimate place, sent her spiralling into a vortex of unspeakable excitement and red-hot, searing pleasure.

She had never been touched like this in her life before and

nothing could have prepared her for the primitive, surging power of her response. When she thought that it was *Luc's* mouth there, caressing her, she wanted to faint.

'I can't wait any longer,' Luc groaned. He entered her, pausing as she automatically flinched. 'You're very tense,' he murmured, looking down at her with a slight frown.

'Please don't stop.' When she opened her eyes and looked at him, she could see the naked hunger as he began to move gently and rhythmically into her.

She shifted under him and with a stifled groan Luc thrust deeper into her, no more able to keep his need for gratification under control than she was.

Having him spill into her, as she peaked with a shuddering orgasm that came in wave upon wave until it finally crested, leaving her limp, gave her the most liberating feeling she had ever experienced.

And afterwards she felt incredibly tired and incredibly peaceful. Luc had rolled onto his back and she could sense him staring up at the ceiling.

Whilst Agatha wanted to curve her body against his and rest her head on his chest so that she could feel the steady beating of his heart, his silence was sending little shards of unease through her.

She thought that this was the definition of reality, this steady drip of icy cold after the hot, euphoric rush.

'That was a mistake,' she whispered. 'You don't have to tell me.' Better to strike first. She forced herself to laugh even though the tingle of awareness that raced through her as he turned to lie on his side, looking at her, gave the lie to any chance of her feeling cool, calm and collected. In fact, now that the memory of what had taken place had its opportunity to cruelly replay itself in her head, she was dimly beginning to recall a certain reluctance on his part to make love to her. Had she thrown herself at him? Had she? She had been feeling miserable and humiliated after the fiasco with Stewart, and there Luc had been, her seemingly never-ending dream-guy, lending her a shoulder to cry on.

Maybe she had even begun to see him as more than just a fantasy when she had started working for him. True, she wasn't on his floor, and most of the time not even within his range of vision, but those snatched occasions when he called her to his office had all done their damage by feeding into her feelings for him. She had interacted with him on a level she had never dreamed possible but, instead of that interaction putting everything into perspective, it had dragged her deeper into her silly infatuation.

And now...

Agatha couldn't bring herself to actually look at him, which was ridiculous, considering her state of complete undress under the duvet.

What must he be thinking? He had been there to comfort her and she had flung herself at him with reckless abandon: what red-blooded male would resist? She could hardly blame him for responding to the invitation. No, she just had to accept that all the blame was squarely on her shoulders.

It seemed very important to salvage some of her pride, at least from the situation.

She clutched the duvet to her chest, suddenly acutely conscious of the body that had thrilled to his touch only moments previously.

'You should go,' she said feverishly.

'We need to talk about what just happened.'

'No, we don't. We really, really don't.' She reluctantly turned to look at him. He had propped himself up on one elbow and the duvet had ridden down to his waist. Her eyes were compulsively drawn to the glorious sight of his exposed chest which in turn triggered off a series of hot little recollections of how that chest had felt under her feverishly exploring hands.

'You were a virgin. Why didn't you tell me?'

'I told you I wasn't experienced. Does it make a difference?' It did; she could read it in his eyes. Her parents had never preached to her, but still she had been raised with high moral values. She had never made a decision to save herself for after marriage, but she had always known that she would save herself for someone she truly cared about. It was just her bad luck that she had picked a man who didn't truly care about her. Her virginity was an embarrassment for him.

'Of course it makes a difference!'

Because what experienced man wants to make love to a woman who hasn't a clue what she's doing?

'Are you going to talk to me? Damn it, Agatha, we at least need to discuss the fact that I didn't use any contraception.'

Agatha blanched in receipt of complications she hadn't even considered. She had been so blown away with passion that the most basic issue of consequences hadn't even begun to surface in her scrambled brain.

'Don't worry.' *Don't worry? Of course he would be worried—sick!* He had slept with her, caught up in the moment just as she had been, but smart enough now that they had exhausted their passion to ask the most fundamental of questions.

'Normally I take responsibility for contraception but this was an event that I didn't foresee.'

'There's no risk of me being pregnant.' She did some quick maths in her head and worked out that she was probably telling the truth. 'So you don't have to add that further worry to the pile. I…I'd like you to go now.'

She would have taken the first step and set an example by getting dressed, but her clothes were on the ground, and covering the short distance with nothing on was too much to bear thinking about.

'Funny, but I'm not believing you. Why did you decide to give your virginity to me?'

'I didn't *decide* anything!' The words were wrenched out of her in her last-ditch attempt to cling on to her dignity. 'It just *happened*. I was really upset over all that business with Stewart and I just wasn't thinking straight. I wasn't thinking at all,' she battled on wretchedly. Nothing in her sheltered life had prepared her for dealing with a situation like this, and it fought against everything in her that compelled her to be honest, but the instinct for survival was stronger. 'I just… fell into bed with you because you were here and I needed comfort.'

'You're telling me that I was *handy*?'

Given a way out, Agatha still shied away from using it. 'I…maybe I don't know.'

'You used me, in other words.'

'Of course I didn't use you.' She was horrified at the picture of herself that those three words conjured up. 'But people just don't think straight when they're upset. And I *was* upset.'

'You barely knew the man!' After an extraordinary high from their love-making, Luc was plummeting back down to earth faster than the speed of light. Since when had he ever been the equivalent of a bottle with which someone could drown their sorrows? If she clutched that damned duvet any tighter around her, she would be in danger of imminent strangulation.

'That's true,' Agatha was forced to concede in a shaky voice. 'But that still doesn't make this right. I'm not, you know, the kind of girl who jumps in the sack with a guy.'

'But you were so overcome with misery after a botched relationship with some loser you knew for all of three minutes that you decided to go for it? Well, on the bright side, at least there won't be any lasting consequences.'

'Sorry?' Her heart skipped a couple of beats as he pushed himself off the bed and began hunting down his clothes. She watched as he walked about the room, drinking in the sight of his magnificent naked body, and trying hard to shut the door on the pernicious shoots of bitter regret trying to eat away at all her good intentions.

She strenuously reminded herself of just how important it was for her not to sink deeper still into her crazy infatuation. Crazy infatuations led to dark, dangerous places. Whilst he was the worst possible candidate for a crush, it would be a disaster were she to fall in love with him. Which she wouldn't, because they were so ill-suited, and because he was just the kind of man mothers warned their daughters about. Except, of course, for *her* mother, who thought the world of him after she had witnessed first-hand his devotion to Danielle and the driven way he had rebuilt her shattered life. He hadn't just restored their family fortunes and beyond, he had restored Danielle's pride.

'Hello? Calling Planet Earth?' Luc strode across to the bed and towered above her, wearing just his boxers. He leaned down, imprisoning her by planting both hands firmly on the bed on either side of her. This was not how the situation should have ended. He was in a filthy mood, and not amused by the way she continued to lie there, taking the blame whilst perversely managing to emerge the wounded party.

He also didn't care for the way his body was hammering at him, telling him that what he really wanted to do was climb back into bed with her and lose himself in her lush, feminine curves. What was going on here?

'I'm sorry.' Agatha reddened, caught out in the act of staring.

'Spare me the apologies. We were talking about consequences—at least there won't be any.' His eyes drifted to her full lips, and then lower, to the soft swell of her breast which she hadn't quite managed to conceal under the duvet. With his self-control threatening to break its leash, Luc dragged his eyes away from the captivating sight. Angry colour scored his fabulous cheekbones. 'The last thing I need is a one-night stand getting pregnant.'

'That's a horrible thing to say.' Agatha felt tears spring at the back of her eyes.

'Why?'

'Because...because it makes me sound cheap.'

'I would lose the moral high-ground, if I were you, considering you've just told me that you used me as a panacea for being in the *dumps*!'

'I'm sorry if you felt insulted. I never meant to hurt you.'

'Hurt me? Since when do you think you're capable of doing that?'

Luc flushed darkly then pushed himself away from the bed to stride over to the window. Even though his good sense was telling him that it was time to go, he was unnerved to find that walking out didn't seem to be that easy.

'And I wasn't using you as a panacea. I'm not that kind of person. Anyway, I don't understand why it would bother you what my reasons were. It's not as though you have lots of morals when it comes to sleeping with women.'

Outraged, Luc looked at her with eyes like black ice. 'I don't believe I'm hearing this.'

Agatha sat up with the duvet still covering her completely and pulled her knees up under it to her chest. She wrapped her arms around her knees and stared at her fingers in mute silence.

'Well? Are you going to explain that remark?'

She started, realising he was now back by the bed, his posture indicative of a man demanding answers. Except she didn't want to answer him. In fact, she wasn't even sure she wanted to speak. She just wanted to dwell on the awful truth that he saw her as a one-night stand, and thankful she was not a one-night stand that would have any lasting repercussions in the form of a pregnancy.

'I get to order all those flowers you send to women you no longer have use for,' she threw at him, suddenly mutinous. 'You don't seem to have a problem with women being handy for *you*.'

'There's an understanding that exists with every woman I have ever slept with.'

'Okay, okay.' The peacemaker in her surfaced.

'I don't encourage longevity,' he rasped harshly. 'That is something that's understood from the starting post.'

Agatha stared at him in stubborn silence and then couldn't stop herself from bursting out, 'I don't understand how you can do that!'

'Not every woman launches into a relationship thinking of marriage and playing happy families,' he said through gritted teeth. His lack of control over proceedings infuriated him.

'No,' she agreed in a tight voice, although she wanted to tell him that he was wrong. There couldn't be a single woman who was overjoyed at the prospect of a pointless fling. Or a one-night stand. Which brought her right back to her own situation and the fact that she had become the one thing she had always thought she wouldn't.

'You are the most frustrating woman I have ever met in my entire life.' Luc swore under his breath.

'You're not accustomed to women having opinions.' She had forgotten about wanting him to leave. The air between them crackled with tension. Every nerve in her body was alive and it was a powerful feeling that sabotaged every scrap of common sense.

'Of course I am. That's the biggest load of rubbish I've ever heard! I meet women in positions of power on a daily basis. We no longer live in the Dark Ages, Agatha. Women have opinions and speak their minds.'

'But not the ones you date!' she flung back, her shimmering turquoise eyes wide and clear as she looked at him.

Was it his imagination or could he see traces of pity there? Was she feeling sorry for him? Shouldn't *he* be the one in that position?

'I don't understand it,' she whispered, forgetting her own misery for a second. 'You've got everything. I mean, you're successful, you're eligible…I know there was all that business with your dad's company, and I know it must have been horribly upsetting for you, knowing that everyone in the town was talking about you, but you came out of it and showed them all. You've done what you wanted to do, you've made pots of money, and Danielle's back in the family home—so how is it that you've never wanted to take the next step and settle down? I know your mum worries about you.'

The sound of her crashing through his personal barriers left him momentarily speechless. Of course, she didn't have a clue that she had done anything wrong. The woman was from another planet. In the space of an hour, she had not only dipped her dainty toe in water no one else had dared tread before, she had dived in headfirst and splashed around!

Rage tried to push through incredulity but failed.

'The ball and chain doesn't quite have enough appeal for me at the moment.' He gathered his self-control with tremendous difficulty. 'So you might as well send that message back to the home front.'

He didn't lose his temper. He never lost his temper. Women never had that effect on him. Occasionally they might irritate, but that was about as far as it ever got. 'And I think this is an appropriate time for me to leave. You're right; mistake made, time to move on.' He began getting dressed.

'I know this probably isn't the right time to bring this up...' Her voice behind him was hesitant. 'But I won't be coming in to work tomorrow. In view of everything that's happened, I'll definitely be resigning. I can post the letter to you, if you want.'

Fear at the thought of not seeing him again tore into her with teeth like razors, but where lay her choice? The possibilities lurking in the aftermath filled her head like a swarm of angry bees. The possibility that her beautiful experience would be his regrettable one, that her role in his life would be reduced to a shaming one-night stand, that she would be forced to retreat to the sidelines and watch as he continued with his life of work and revolving women, that he would not be able to look at her without pity and contempt... Each seemed worse than the one before, and doubly worse when she thought about carrying on in her job, viewing it all first-hand and on a daily basis.

'We've covered the resignation issue,' Luc informed her flatly.

Hassle in his private life was not something he tolerated. Yes, he went out with arm candy, and sure he could understand why his mother might find that a little alarming, but arm candy didn't stress him out. *This* stressed him out. Of course she wanted to scarper. She had leapt into bed with him, and she needn't have told him that it probably would have amounted to the biggest mistake of her life as far as she was concerned. She wasn't a one-night stand kind of girl. Referring to her in that manner had been a low blow, he admitted to himself, but he wasn't going to apologise.

Nor was he going to give her the easy way out and allow her to walk away without due procedure.

'Yes, well, that was before we...'

'Rules are rules. You have to give notice. What happened in this bedroom has nothing to do with work. I don't play by those rules.'

'But—'

'I also doubt the Employment Tribunal would take a lenient view if I sacked employees at the drop of a hat. Instant dismissal is only relevant in certain circumstances. Yours doesn't fall into that category.'

'But it's going to be awkward.' She could feel herself perspiring under the duvet, and the treacherous pull of her body towards him as though she was being tugged by an invisible line, yanked in a direction she wanted to run from.

'Is it? I thought what happened was just a simple mistake that we were going to put behind us.'

'Yes,' Agatha confirmed hurriedly. 'Yes, of course.' Already he had moved on and was tackling the situation like the experienced man of the world that he was. While she clutched a quilt, got knots in her tummy thinking about her 'one-night stand' label and tried to downplay the horror of still being in his company—thinking about him while he carried on with life as though nothing had happened, following her instructions, which would be easy for him, but hellish for her. Who knew? In two weeks' time, she might even be out buying some high-wattage trinket for another of his women.

'So what's the problem?'

'No problem.'

'And,' he continued coolly, 'don't get it into your head that I'm going to have to answer for you leaving my company. I won't. When you leave, you'll explain to your mother that you left because you couldn't hack it. You'll be back to square one, jobless in Yorkshire, which isn't my problem. I won't take the blame for that situation.'

'No. Of course not,' Agatha said faintly. Her mother would be bitterly disappointed. There were no jobs to be had locally. For Agatha not even to have stuck it out for a year would seem like ingratitude, to someone who had elevated Luc to the status of a saint following the way he had taken care of his mother. He had uttered nothing to the press but to promise that the finance director would be buried for what he had done, and he had silenced wagging tongues with the sheer force of his personality. He had made sure to be a presence in the village and had let it be known, by virtue of the odd throwaway remark, that he would be merciless towards anyone who failed to support his mother.

There had been no need to adopt that approach; Danielle had always been a popular member of the community, contributing to the church fairs, helping out at fundraisers and opening the house and grounds once a year so that everyone could enjoy a summer party at their expense.

Both Agatha and her mother had been deeply impressed by the commanding way he had taken care of the situation.

Agatha now thought that she could probably find another word to describe his approach. Maybe 'high-handed'. Maybe 'arrogant'. But Edith would never believe that. She would be left with the impression that her daughter had packed in a golden opportunity because she couldn't be bothered to try hard enough.

'I could always keep looking for another job in London,' she whispered.

'Doing what? You've hardly proved yourself working for me, and what would you expect me to do about your reference?'

'My reference?'

'Well, what have you proved to me? That you have no self-motivation, no enthusiasm to try for the career ladder, open boredom with everything to do with office work.' Luc scarcely recognised his intractability. Shouldn't *he* be the one shedding the problem as fast as he could? Confusion at his own inexplicable reactions conspired to fill him with burning rage at himself.

'In other words, you'd make sure that I was unemployable in London just because we fell into bed for all the wrong reasons, and because I'm not one of those women who think it's okay to carry on falling into bed just for a bit of fun.'

'Do you really think that I'm petty enough to resort to those kinds of tactics because you've decided to play the distraught, outraged maiden?' Luc's lip curled and her eyes fluttered away from his.

If you can't take the heat, she thought, *then get out of the kitchen.* A man like Luc, a predator who ruthlessly took what he wanted out of life, wasn't going to tiptoe around her, making room for her insecurities and doubts. Lord only knew how many women he had slept with, and he had no scruples when those women outstayed their welcome.

How could she have thought that she could dump her sheltered upbringing, her morals and principles and sleep with him when she had had first-hand experience of how he treated women? How could she have been stupid enough to imagine that dreams could turn into ongoing reality?

She had built a lot of idealised fairy-tale castles in her head and she had no one else to blame because they had been exposed for what they were.

He strolled towards her and every slow step threatened her already shattered peace of mind.

'You need to start asking yourself a few questions,' he said, his voice deadly soft. 'You might waffle on until the day you die about climbing into bed with me because you were suffering some terrible bout of temporary insanity, but when you looked at me I was seeing a very different story. You *wanted* me. So why don't you be honest with yourself and cut to the chase? We didn't have sex because you weren't thinking straight. We had sex because you *wanted* it.' He felt driven to hear her admit it.

Agatha stared at him in mute silence. She could feel anger roiling just below his cold exterior and she wondered if he thought that she was playing games with him.

'No woman comes on to a man the way you did because she's a little upset and needs a bit of company.'

'I didn't come on to you.'

Luc gave a shout of mirthless laughter. 'You might make a big song and dance about the way I treat women, Agatha, but at the very least I don't have a problem with honesty. If all you wanted was a pat on the back and a shoulder to cry on, you would have run screaming the second you knew I was going to kiss you. You didn't. In fact, I seem to recall...'

'No!'

Luc looked at her for a long while, then he offered an indifferent shrug. 'Don't you like thinking that you might have physical needs like any other woman?' His expression was veiled but there was nothing veiled about what he was doing to her, forcing her to confront her sexuality, throwing all her moans and whimpers of encouragement back in her face.

How tedious he must have found it, when he would be used to women who knew what they were doing in bed.

'I know I have physical needs,' Agatha whispered. At least, she did now, and the power and urgency of them terrified her.

'Now we're getting somewhere,' Luc's voice was laced with thick sarcasm.

'And it's wonderful!' she said with a bright, defensive

smile. 'And you're right, it's silly to hide behind excuses. I made love to you because I wanted to.'

Luc had lost count of the number of women who had been eager to tell him how much they wanted him. When Agatha had said it, in the heat of the moment, with the roar of passion in her ears, he had liked it. It had turned him on. He liked this even more, hearing her say it again but in the cool aftermath of sex.

There was just something so incredibly sexy about her tousled innocence and the knowledge that she had lost her virginity to him. He could hardly believe how much he wanted to savour the thought of that. It was like she had managed to dig deep inside him and pull out a primal instinct he was hardly aware of possessing.

Let her confront her own mixed-up responses, he thought. He might just wait for her to say what he knew she would— that there had never been any question of her throwing herself at him because he had just happened to be there, right time, right place.

He wasn't given to waiting for women. But, yes, he might make an exception in this case, because when he thought of those big, rosy nipples and the voluptuous, silky-smooth curves of her body, his body went into overdrive.

'See?' he drawled lazily, watching her through shuttered eyes. 'How hard was that? Ten out of ten for facing up to reality.'

Agatha fought a tide of burning resentment.

'If I can feel this way with you,' she told him fiercely, 'then how much more wonderful will it be when I make love to a man who means something to me? So you've won. I'm not sorry we made love and I'm not ashamed either. I know my virginity would have been a turn-off for you. Men like you want experienced women who don't go into meltdown after they've made love. But there's a man out there for me, and I feel so much more confident now that I'll find him.'

CHAPTER FIVE

AGATHA had not been foolish enough to put any faith in the remainder of the evening to somehow miraculously put things into perspective and to fill her with a bracing optimism to face the next day, back at work after the shattering events of Sunday.

However, she was dismayed to find that no amount of stern lecturing of herself or level-headed reasoning could take away the sickening knot in her stomach as she stood in front of the gleaming lift doors, waiting for it to carry her up to her cubby hole.

She had given an awful lot of house room to the idea of hibernating in her room until her notice was up, but then that would have allowed the one-off episode with Luc to dictate her behaviour, and she didn't want that. She had spent way too long with a bunch of silly, girlhood fantasies for company and, now that those fantasies had become a very unlikely reality, she wasn't about to let them take over the role of running her emotional life.

She also wasn't going to dress like a refugee from a charity shop. She had reluctantly admitted to herself that one very good thing seemed to have come of her recklessness with Luc: she no longer felt self-conscious of her body. She had seen genuine, hot appreciation in his eyes when he had looked at her, and for the first time in her life her curves had not been a source of embarrassment. She had wantonly revelled in the attention they had provoked, and miraculously the feeling had stayed with her.

So instead of her grey, woollen skirt and blouse, and the all-encompassing cardigan which was as unflattering as it was comfortable, she pulled out the few items of clothing she possessed that were relatively fitted and suitable for work: a slim-fitting black skirt and a plain but figure-hugging cream, long-sleeved jumper. The paisley-patterned scarf, given to her by her mother as a 'you're starting work in a proper job in an office' gift, was pulled out of hibernation from a box at the bottom of her wardrobe and added vibrant colour to the outfit.

As she walked to her little office, she knew that she was getting quite a bit of attention. In fact, with a spontaneity she didn't know she possessed, she actually grinned and turned around to blow her colleague Adrian an air kiss when he wolf whistled as she passed his desk.

More than anything, she wished that she was working in the central hub of the office, where the buzz of telephones and light-hearted banter between phone calls and computer work might have distracted her from her thoughts.

Her own desk, tucked away along the corridor, could be seen as either a haven of solitude or a miserable and isolated cage. She wondered whether Personnel had stuck her out of the way because, with her limited experience, she would have been a disadvantage to all the bright young things with their degrees and top-notch computer skills. At the time, she had been told that, because she would be working more or less directly with Luc, she might occasionally be passed something of a reasonably confidential nature and so a private space would be more acceptable. Belatedly she realised that indeed she did handle some confidential stuff, if you could call dealing with his girlfriends confidential.

She pushed open the door to her little office, turned automatically to the coat hook hanging on the wall by the side of the door and was only aware of the presence of someone else in the room when she was ready to head towards her desk. Only to find Luc perched on it, his hands lightly clasped on his lap.

Agatha couldn't have received a bigger shock if she had discovered an alien at her computer terminal. Of course, she had expected to bump into him at some point in time, but not just yet. Not when she had barely had time to recover her lost equilibrium.

She stood in awkward, gaping silence for a few seconds, then stammered, 'Wh-what are you doing here?' It was an uphill struggle to remember that she was turning over a new leaf, valiantly jettisoning all the shackles that had held her down.

'I own the company. Remember? I have a right to be anywhere I want to be.'

'Yes, but…'

'But life would have been more comfortable for you if I'd been polite enough to keep out of sight until your notice was up and you could slink away unobserved?'

Agatha didn't say anything, because he had hit the nail on the head, although the prickly, heightened feeling running riot inside her now made her wonder whether her addiction to him wouldn't find her seeking him out on some pretext or other. Bad habits were difficult to stamp out.

Luc looked at her with a shuttered expression but his sharp eyes were taking everything in. He had had the rest of the evening to think about her parting shot, and the sexy little outfit she was wearing now proclaimed a sexually awakened woman on the move. A woman *he* had wakened. On the move for another man.

He wasn't ready for that yet. He also wasn't prepared to let his work suffer because his mind kept straying to one night of white-hot passion, but suffer it had. Yesterday evening, he had done the unthinkable and jeopardised a deal, albeit a small one, because he hadn't been able to focus on the finer details of the company accounts on his computer. He had only been able to salvage the mess by the skin of his teeth.

Agatha was unfinished business and that was a situation that wasn't going to work.

Every situation had its solution. In this case, the solution lay in getting her back to bed—warm, willing and of her own volition. Whether she knew it or not, it would work for both of them because, if she was his unfinished business, then he was hers. Until this was sorted, she would interrupt his work and he would interrupt her head. And, yes, it went against everything inside him to pursue this situation but the need to pursue was overpowering. He was going to throw the rule book through the window. He could only think that it was because he still wanted her and getting what he wanted was too ingrained in him to be ignored.

'Unfortunately for you, I've done a bit of thinking,' he continued, standing up and strolling to the single window that overlooked the busy pavements below. He turned back around to look at her. 'You might just get it into your head that you can slack off because you intend to leave.'

'I wouldn't do that!' Agatha protested vehemently.

'Really? Then explain the outfit. Not what I would call suitable, would you?'

'I'm only wearing what every other female under forty in this building wears!' Agatha defended herself stoutly, while making small movements to tug down the skirt which was a hefty couple of inches above the knee. 'And you told me to change my wardrobe,' she carried on, emboldened.

Privately, Luc had to concede that she had a point, but

for some reason it annoyed the hell out of him to see her flaunting herself in clothes that would bring most men to a grinding halt. Did she really expect to go unnoticed every time she left her office to run some errand that would take her past the boys working in the outer offices? Of course not. But then that was probably the intention.

'The fact is that I find myself in an unusual position,' he informed her, walking towards her, then circling like a shark sizing up edible prey. 'Having made it a rule never to sleep with an employee, I now discover that breaking the rule carries consequences. I've opened a door that you could enter to do any number of things if you decided to take revenge for being a one-night stand. Even if you *were* the one to instigate the situation.' He scowled, grimly disappointed with himself for breaking his own iron-clad code of conduct.

'I'm not into revenge! Why do you always suspect the worst of people?'

'Call it dealing with the daily reality of being wealthy. I've had more than one threat of a kiss-and-tell story. Personally, I'm indifferent to that, but my mother gets upset.'

'Do you really think that I'm the sort of girl who would do that?'

'I don't know.' He gave an elegant shrug. 'I never thought that you were the sort of girl to jump in the sack for a session of hot sex and then decide to use it as a springboard.'

Agatha flushed to the roots of her hair. She bitterly regretted those last words. They had made her sound cheap and shallow and she couldn't blame him now for thinking the worst of her.

'Because I've decided to wear normal clothes to work, doesn't mean that I'm going to put my feet up on the desk and slack off.'

He noticed that she had said nothing to defend herself

against his accusation. A lethal fury swept through him, unlike anything he had ever felt before, but none of that was reflected in his face.

'Other things come into play here,' he informed her in a grim undertone while she looked up at him in utter bemusement.

'What other things?'

'I don't care for the thought of you shooting your mouth off and discussing what took place between us.'

'You can trust me when I tell you that that's the last thing I would ever think of doing and, just in case you don't believe me, I'll happily make a deal with you. I don't say a word to anyone, and you don't.' Thoughts of her mother's disappointed face made her shudder.

'I don't do deals.' That little shudder of hers hadn't escaped his notice. 'On the other hand, I *can* make sure that I keep an eye on you.'

'Keep an eye on me?' Agatha parroted, trying to make some kind of connection in her head that would give her some insight into what he was trying to tell her.

'Your time in this little box is at an end. For the remainder of your employment here, you'll be on my floor, sitting outside my office, where I'll have ample opportunity to make sure that you're not putting your feet up. I'll also be able to make sure that you're not whiling away your time gossiping.'

Agatha's mouth dropped open and her brain braked and then slowed to a standstill before cranking back into gear. Very slowly.

'You can't be serious.'

'Never been more serious in my life. I have a reputation to protect and I intend to make sure that you don't damage it.'

'It's not as though everyone doesn't know that...'

'I don't care who knows that I play the field.' Luc helped her out, his tone dismissive. 'I do, however, care that they don't know I've been crazy enough to play the field right in my own back yard.' Only he was capable of recognising the subtle but important distinction, which was that for the first time he was willing to play the field in his own back yard.

Agatha's mind latched on to that single word 'crazy'. She wanted to tell him that she had been the crazy one ever to have allowed herself the folly of falling into his arms as if her entire life had been building up to that very moment. Instead, she resolved there and then to do everything within her power to wipe him out of her head.

She took a few shaky steps away from him towards her desk and then turned to him with a sullen shrug.

'You already have a secretary.'

'Helen's daughter has just had her second child. She would welcome a break of a few weeks. I had planned on asking my agency to send a temp over, but in all events this is a far more satisfactory solution.' And one that had occurred to him on the spur of the moment. He could only sardonically admire his talent for creativity when it came to breaking his own rules so that he could invent a couple of new ones.

'I'm not really qualified to do Helen's job.' With ever-vanishing hope, Agatha clung to that observation with the tenacity of a drowning swimmer clinging to a life belt, but in her heart she knew that it was a pretty futile hope. He was a deeply suspicious man in a situation over which he fancied he lacked total control. How wrong he was!

'She'll spend the next couple of days filling you in and I'll handle anything sensitive.'

'Will that include buying presents for your lovers?' She pressed her hand to her mouth as if she could somehow stuff the words back in and swallow them down.

Luc looked at her narrowly, eyes gleaming. When he took

one step towards her, Agatha instinctively fell back. 'Would that bother you? Would you be jealous?'

'No!'

A slow smile curved his sexy mouth and he dropped his eyes, which actually didn't do very much to release her from her semi-frozen, trance-like state. 'Well,' he drawled. 'You'll be thrilled to hear that I won't be calling on you to do that.'

Did that mean that he would recommence his high-octane love life, just omitting her from the responsibility of buying gifts, reserving restaurants and seats at operas? she wondered feverishly, and then was ashamed of letting her thoughts go down that pointless road.

'And look on the bright side. There's another reason why you should applaud my decision to bring you to the director's floor. If you decide to go into another office job after this, you'll want a good reference. Work for me and come up to scratch, and you'll be in demand the second you leave this building. All told, you can see that I'm doing you a favour.'

'Your favours never feel like favours,' Agatha breathed on a rebellious sigh.

Mutual attraction, the brief game of pursuit and capture then gratification. That was the course of events he had always followed with women, and after the gratification came the gratitude. He was cynical enough to know that he was a catch, maybe one of the biggest in the sea.

Agatha had turned that normal course of events on its head. Was that why he was driven to get her back in his bed at all costs and even at the expense of his fabled self-control?

At any rate, he sucked in his breath sharply and said with curt self-restraint, 'Come up to the director's floor when you've cleared your desk. I'll be out for the remainder of the day, but Helen will show you the ropes.'

Which, Agatha supposed as she trudged with her possessions up the lift to the plush glass-house occupied by the high and mighty at the top of the building, was something.

And at least she would be doing some real work; there was always a positive spin to be put on everything, she told herself. Also, Luc had been right: he would be able to dispatch her with reasonable references if she left with more experience, and that would mean something to him. It would reduce any residue of guilt that the job he had been forced to provide for her hadn't worked out.

As she might have expected, he had taken a pragmatic view of what had happened. Whilst she had spent the weekend unable to function, he had worked out how to make sure she was dispatched in a way that would protect his privacy and preserve his conscience.

Helen's office was private and luxurious, glass and chrome, with an adjoining door to Luc's bigger, even more luxurious office. In between being shown the systems, she played with the thought that maybe seeing Luc on a daily basis would go somewhere to getting him out of her system. Didn't familiarity breed contempt? There was never a person who longed for that as much as she did.

For the next week and a half, it really seemed to be working—in a manner of speaking. Because Luc, in full throttle, had to be seen to be believed. However early she made it to the office, he was always there before her. She brought him in a cup of coffee, and then life immediately went into the fast lane.

Even with his feet up on his desk, his tie askew, his mind was still working at such a rapid speed that she was barely able to take time out to breathe, never mind pander to the temptation to sit back and just look at him.

'Got that?'

With an efficiency Agatha would never have believed possible after the computer course she just scraped through months ago, she nodded and stood up, smoothing down her skirt in the process. When her eyes flicked to him, it was to find him staring at her with that speculative intensity that made the hairs on the back of her neck stand on end. Over the past week and a half, he had treated her with the scrupulous detachment of the boss towards his secretary. Now, as the clock ticked towards lunch time, he was finally looking at her, and all the nervousness that had been resting happily on the back burner bubbled up to the surface with ferocious speed.

'You've certainly been hiding your light under a bushel,' he drawled, pushing back his chair and then folding his hands behind his head. 'For someone in love with the outdoor life, who hated anything to do with the office, you seem to be keeping up.'

Agatha could feel his cool, inscrutable eyes resting on her, and her heart did that hammering thing that always seemed to turn her brain to mush. Had she really kidded herself that she was somehow over him because she had been able to handle working alongside him without falling apart from nerves?

The prospect of being back at square one hit her like a punch in the stomach. Despite all her good intentions, she had done nothing to move on with her love life. She could see the possibility of becoming ensconced in this new, temporary position, which was doing nothing to promote the contempt she had been waiting for—the opposite, in fact—and then feeling the separation when she finally did leave even more than she would have bargained for.

The small shoots of a plan began to form in her head and she glumly gave it room while the man who still spiked her dreams continued to look at her with that mild, dispassionate interest.

'I don't have much choice, do I?' She held his stare and tried not to fiddle with her fingers. 'Anyway, I am kind of enjoying the work,' she admitted truthfully. 'It's much more interesting than the stuff I was doing downstairs.'

'Not my fault. You came to me without much going for you by way of experience in even the most lowly of office skills, and you never showed any interest in furthering your knowledge. How was I to know that you were such a quick study?'

Agatha flushed with pleasure at the compliment.

'I've had a number of temps over the years,' Luc said, musing. 'And none of them have matched you for efficiency. In fact, a number of them fell to pieces the minute the going got a little tough.'

Agatha had no trouble believing that. She, at least, had known the nature of the beast and had adapted accordingly. Luc was brilliant, relentless, impatient with mistakes and never expected to explain anything more than once. Glimpses of his character over the years had stood her in good stead.

'Poor things,' she said sympathetically, visualising a procession of weeping, broken young girls.

'Poor things?' Luc laughed, folded his hands behind his head. 'I am the most considerate employer anyone could wish for.'

'Really?'

'Yes. Really. You seem to have managed perfectly.' He paused significantly. 'Do you think that might have something to do with our special relationship?' He trained his sharp, green eyes on her, enjoying the sight: pink cheeks, that full mouth and curly blond hair half-escaping the loose bun at the nape of her neck. Working with her was a constant challenge to suppress his rampant libido. Moreover, and to his surprise, he had quickly discovered that he had acquired a top-rate worker who was much brighter and cleverer than she gave herself credit for. He considered her wasted talking to plants in some tin-pot garden centre, but he would approach his offer to keep her on in a brand-new position later.

For the moment, he was frustrated by cravings over which he seemed to have little control. Even when he was safely out of her radius and in meetings, he had still found his concentration lapsing.

Playing the waiting game was not in his nature and he knew, more positively with each passing hour, that he needed to get a conclusion going.

'We don't have a special relationship,' Agatha said crisply.

'We had sex. Don't tell me you've forgotten. Some might say that qualifies us as having a special relationship.' He sat forward, resting both elbows on his highly polished desk and afforded her a penitent look. 'My apologies. Talking about sex in a working environment is inappropriate. What *is* appropriate,' he continued, 'Is I take you out to lunch. You deserve it; point taken that I may not always be the easiest person to work with.'

'That's very nice, thank you, but I've got some stuff I need to do at lunch time.'

Luc frowned. 'What sort of stuff? I'm the boss. I'm giving you full permission to ignore work for an hour and a half.'

'Actually, I wasn't going to work.'

'What exactly are you planning on doing? You have to eat.'

'I've brought some sandwiches in. I...I have some things

to do on the computer. Emails to write, if that's okay. Keeping in touch! I told mum that I would probably be handing in my notice and she's worried.'

'Right. Maybe another day.'

'Maybe...' Agatha looked away. 'So...is that all?'

Luc had never felt so instantly dispatched. For someone who gave the impression of being a pushover, she was as tough as nails, he thought with ill humour. What email could be so pressing that she would give up lunch with him?

'I won't be here this afternoon.' Frustration ratcheted through him as he walked over to the cupboard in which his jacket was hanging. 'Wall-to-wall meetings until six. I'll expect that due-diligence report to be completed by the time I return to the office. If it's not, you'll have to work overtime. The lawyers need it first thing in the morning.'

'Of course.' She sprang to her feet. 'Anything else?'

'That's a rather open-ended question. What did you have in mind?' He enjoyed the way she went bright red at that. His sharp eyes took in the way she stuck her hands behind her back, as though scared that they might somehow betray her, the way her pupils dilated and the way her breathing quickened. Under the polished veneer, she was still as much a prisoner to that one explosive night as he was.

'I'll see you tomorrow,' he drawled, leaving her with a backward wave of his hand.

Agatha breathed a sigh of heartfelt relief as the door closed behind him. What had he been playing at with those references to sex? Had he found it entertaining to confuse her?

With a burst of sudden determination, and a few surreptitious glances around her just in case the walls really did have eyes, she spent the next fifteen minutes surfing the Internet in search of online dating sites. It was not something she enjoyed doing but this, apparently, was the way things got done if you didn't have the sort of extensive social life that promoted lots of face-to-face meetings with exciting, eligible guys. And what harm could there be in it? She didn't really hold out much hope for finding the man of her dreams, but she might meet some interesting people. Having come to the decision that she would not return to rural Yorkshire, but instead stay where she was and try her best to hunt down another job, a few new faces might be just the thing.

She would not become her own worst enemy by allowing the debacle with Stewart to push her into self-defensive, wary reclusivity from which she would have all the time in the world to devote her thoughts to her one-night stand with Luc. She positively needed the distraction of another guy.

She registered at the biggest site. Then, in an upbeat mood, she went to the company restaurant for lunch, ignoring the limp sandwiches in her desk in favour of a more celebratory meal of spaghetti Bolognese, followed by fudge cake and lots of interesting chats with the friends she had left several floors below. It was funny to think that Luc was actually wary about her spilling the beans on their one-night affair. To become a prime target for gossip was probably the last thing in the world Agatha would ever have wanted.

Four hours later, she was leaving the impressive glass building when Luc stepped in front of her, blocking her path. She hadn't seen him, hadn't heard him. He was as light as a panther on his feet. And he didn't look in the best of moods.

'I did what you asked. I finished the due-diligence report. It's on your desk.'

'Fun lunch?'

'Sorry?' She stopped and looked at him cautiously.

'How are you getting back to your bedsit?'

'Tube,' Agatha said faintly. 'Then bus.'

Luc didn't answer. He stretched out one hand and miraculously a black cab appeared.

'I can't afford to take a cab to—'

'Get in the taxi, Agatha.'

'Are you all right? You don't look too good. Are you feeling all right?'

Luc didn't trust himself to say anything and that was a new experience for him. He waited until she was inside the taxi, then he lowered himself next to her, breaking his silence only to give the taxi driver directions to her house.

Agatha glanced across at his exquisite profile and stuttered into nervous speech, relaying calls he had received during his absence and progress she had made with a midsized publishing company in which Luc was interested. The company had fired Agatha's interest because it specialised in gardening books. Anxiously aware that her babbling seemed to be falling on deaf ears, but unwilling to spend the rest of the car drive in complete silence stewing in her own confusion and alarm, she instead chose to chatter on about ideas she had for rejuvenating the company.

'What's the matter?' she asked eventually. 'I mean, why are you coming back with me to my flat? I'm perfectly capable of getting there on my own. I don't need you to babysit me. I thought we'd talked this through.'

'I'm not sure we've talked it through enough.' Luc turned in his seat and looked at her with blazing intensity. 'Tell me how else you occupied yourself today. Feel free to skip the riveting conversations with clients.'

Agatha broke out in clammy, nervous perspiration. Not even the taxi pulling up outside her flat could save her from the necessity of answering because it quickly became apparent that he intended to escort her into her bedsit. She was like someone under house arrest.

'Well, what do you want to hear?' She turned on him the

second they were inside her little sitting area, hands on her hips, her blue eyes bright with anger. It wasn't fair that he should be here, crowding her space when all she wanted to do was recover from the effects of him.

'Okay, so I didn't have those sandwiches at my desk. I went to the canteen because I fancied a bit of company. And, before you accuse me of gossiping, I didn't say a word about…anything.'

'I returned to the office shortly after I left. I'd forgotten some reports.'

Agatha looked at him blankly.

'The reports were on your desk. You were at lunch.'

He strolled to the window, not for the first time thinking that her landlord should be shot. When he slowly turned round to look at her, it was to find that she had not moved from her hesitant position by the door, although she had removed her coat and placed it on the arm of the sofa.

'I don't see why I should feel guilty because I went to the office canteen for lunch,' Agatha muttered in a moment of rebellion. 'You can't keep an eye on me a hundred percent of the time, and if you've come here to haul me over the coals for nothing then please just go. I'm really tired.' She took a couple of steps and flopped wearily down onto the sofa, briefly closing her eyes and allowing the weight of everything to settle on her shoulders.

'You left your computer running when you went to lunch.' Luc walked towards her and remained towering over her until she opened reluctant eyes to look at him.

'Did I?'

'You should really close all tabs when you're on the Internet browsing through dating sites.'

It took a few seconds for the significance of his words to sink in, then she sat bolt-upright and clenched her fists at her sides.

SAVE OVER £39

25% OFF

Sign up to get 4 stories a month for 12 months in advance and **SAVE £39.60 – that's a fantastic 25% off**
If you prefer you can sign up for 6 months in advance and **SAVE £15.84 – that's still an impressive 20% off**

FULL PRICE	PER-PAID SUBSCRIPTION PRICE	SAVINGS	MONTHS
£158.40	£118.80	25%	12
£79.20	£63.36	20%	6

- **FREE P&P** Your books will be delivered direct to your door every month for FREE

- **Plus** to say thank you, we will send you a **FREE L'Occitane gift set worth over £10**
  Gift set has a RRP of £10.50 and includes Verbena Shower Gel 75m and Soap 110g

What's more you will receive ALL of these additional benefits

- Be the FIRST to receive the most up-to-date titles
- FREE P&P
- Lots of free gifts and exciting special offers
- Monthly exclusive newsletter
- Special REWARDS programme
- No Obligation –
  You can cancel your subscription at any time by writing to us at Mills & Boon Book Club, PO Box 676, Richmond, TW9 1WU.

MILLS & BOON®

Sign up to save online at www.millsandboon.co.uk

P1AIT

'You were *snooping* around on my computer?'

Luc had the grace to flush but an apology couldn't have been further from his mind. 'I wanted to check and make sure that all the relevant documents had been downloaded before I wasted another journey. Checking them on your computer saved me the effort of going into my office. I use the word *your* with reservations—let's not forget that the computer actually belongs to the company, and by extension to me.'

Agatha sighed with a growing sense of defeat. 'Okay. Now you know and it's no big deal. It's the modern way of meeting people.'

'It's the modern way of getting into trouble.' He could have kicked himself for waiting for her to come to him. While he had been playing the waiting game, she had been scouring the Internet to find men. He should damn well have obeyed his finely tuned hunting instincts. They had always worked for him in the past.

This woman challenged every ounce of control he had ever mistakenly assumed he had, and it all came down to one thing: lust. If he had suspected her of playing games with him, he would have had no trouble in walking away. If—unlikely though it might be—she genuinely didn't fancy him, then he would likewise have shrugged his shoulders and put it down to one of life's little experiences. But, against all odds, Agatha both wanted to walk away *and* fancied him like mad. The combination was driving him crazy, but not as crazy as he had been when he had innocently come upon that website listing so-called eligible men.

Privately, Agatha agreed that Internet dating probably wasn't for her. In fact, as the afternoon had progressed, her optimistic thoughts about meeting interesting people via a dating site had begun to lose its appeal. By the time Luc had blocked her path outside the office, she had already come to the conclusion that she must have been suffering from temporary insanity to have cooked up the idea in the first place.

Not that she intended to admit that.

'I think you'll find that some dating agencies have an excellent record in successful partnerships.'

'Really? Is that what you were hoping for? A successful partnership?'

Agatha was busy reading the cynicism behind that pithy little question and wasn't liking it. Did he think that she was incapable of finding a lifelong partner, even on a dating site?

'These things *do* happen!' she snapped, red-faced and flustered. 'Although,' she admitted with wrenching honesty, 'I did think that it would be nice to meet a few new faces before I start looking around for another job.'

Some nice, new, shiny, bright young men who might make me forget you. She couldn't look at him. The silence grew and grew, and she really didn't know what to do with it, because her head was in a whirl and self-pity was beginning to gnaw away at her insides.

'I don't like the thought of you meeting new faces,' Luc intoned bluntly.

That brought Agatha's head snapping up and she stared at him in open-mouthed surprise. 'You don't like the thought of me meeting guys? Are you *jealous*?' She couldn't believe how quickly the empty feeling inside her was replaced by a soaring sensation of delight—which was short-lived, as Luc granted her a look of harsh incredulity.

'Jealous?' He gave a bark of laughter. 'I have never been jealous in my life!' But thinking of her even casting her eyes in another direction *did* subject him to a tide of blinding rage.

He had no problem accepting this fact, because he was

a possessive man, and there was nothing wrong with that. But jealous? No way.

'No, you're not.' Agatha dully corrected her over-optimistic interpretation. 'You still think that you need to look out for me, because if I could get taken in by a creep like Stewart Dexter then who knows how many other creeps lurking on the Internet can pull the wool over my eyes?'

Luc, still standing and commanding every ounce of her unwilling attention, finally lowered his stunning eyes and drawled in that low, lazy voice that could send her into reckless free fall, 'No new men, Agatha. You and I—we have unfinished business. We're not putting it behind us and pretending it never happened. It happened and it's going to happen again. Because it's what we both want.'

CHAPTER SIX

AGATHA was mesmerised by the rich, velvety conviction of his voice.

'No, you're wrong,' she protested weakly.

'But when I make love to you, I want to do it in comfort. This bedsit is not comfortable.' Luc overrode her feeble denial with ease. 'We'll go back to my place.'

'That's crazy!'

'Nice king-sized bed.' He strode towards her bedroom, literally a matter of a few steps, and began hunting around for some kind of overnight bag. 'Bathroom with every modern convenience known to man.' He flung some random clothes on the bed, while Agatha looked at him, stupefied and lulled into immobility. Vague, nebulous thoughts of her optimistic 'moving on' process tried and failed to take shape.

'The finest rugs, a kitchen with a fridge that actually works, plasma TV—although I don't plan on either of us sitting in front of it...' More clothes joined the ones piling up in disarray.

'What are you *doing*?' She leapt off the sofa and watched as he opened and closed drawers.

'I'm taking control.'

'Shut that drawer!'

He reached inside and pulled out an assortment of over-sized tee-shirts, holding them up for inspection before tossing them right back into the drawer. 'Sleepwear? Never mind. You won't be needing those.'

'We can't do this!' she screeched in an agonised voice.

'Why not?' His eyes clashed with her, vibrant and simmering. 'Are you going to tell me that you don't want me to make love to you? For hours? Touch you where I know you like to be touched? Lick you in places that make you squirm and beg for more?'

Agatha was squirming now, imagining all those things she had tried to firmly shut the door on. 'No. Maybe...I don't know!'

'That's okay because I know for the both of us. Feel free to stop agonising.' He walked towards her and cupped her upturned face in one hand, then he slowly lowered his head. He met with no resistance. Instead of listening to his pride and stepping back, maybe this was what he should have done all along—forced the issue caveman-style. Lord, but it felt good.

Agatha felt his mouth claim hers and she surrendered with a shameful lack of restraint, her arms reaching up to link behind his neck as though he might disappear in a puff of smoke if she didn't hold on hard to him.

Everything he had said was true. He was her irresistible passion. If he was only in it for the sex, then why shouldn't she at least take what was on offer and enjoy it while it lasted instead of making a martyr out of herself? Self-sacrifice might be noble and worthy but since when did it make a good bed companion?

Travelling back to his house with her overnight bag was unbearably exciting. Even the composed tenor of his conversation in the back seat of the black taxi fanned the flames, because underneath the light banter she could smell the hunger inside him, and it matched hers.

When they finally made it to his penthouse suite, she was ready to explode.

She was aware of very modern, neutral surroundings. Pale wooden floors covered an expanse that was vast by London standards and, sure enough, she glimpsed those magnificent rugs he had mentioned, and also huge statement-piece abstract paintings which he hadn't mentioned.

But then, after those initial moments of sanity, she was swept away on a tide of passion. At some point she knew that her clothes were off and she was on a huge bed, watching as he undressed and closed the curtains. She was so aroused by the sight of him that she had to lightly touch herself, and when he moved to stand naked in front of her, looking down and smiling, she whimpered and allowed him to complete what she had begun.

Entangled between sheets that felt like satin, and which ended up half off the bed, Agatha opened herself up to the joy of being touched by his hands, his fingers, his mouth. It all felt so *right*.

For the first time, she confronted her emotions with honesty and realised that her feelings for Luc weren't just lust. Yes, maybe they once were, but gradually she had fallen in love with the man as opposed to having fallen in lust with the one-dimensional cut-out.

When she curled her fingers into his springy black hair, and watched through half-opened eyes as he feasted on her breasts, she allowed herself the luxury of letting her love show, because he couldn't see it.

To let him witness how she really felt about him would be a sure-fire way of making him disappear as fast as he could over the horizon.

But still… She could dream, couldn't she?

When later, she was lying tucked against him, he told her that that was the best sex he had ever had, she smiled and filed the compliment away. When later still, after they had made love again, he turned to face her and said seriously that she should reconsider handing in her notice, she filed that away too under the optimistic heading of 'he can't bear the thought of being too far away from me.'

'The situation has changed,' Luc murmured, surprising himself, because having his lover working for him was far from ideal. In fact, it was downright awkward, but the thought of her finding a job in another company made his blood run cold. How long before some office lothario decided that she was fair game? The woman was sexy as hell, and she was bright too. There would be no back room for her in which to hide away from men with their eyes popping out of their heads.

Luc conceded to himself that he might possibly be jealous.

'I know.' Agatha trailed her fingers across his broad shoulders, then rested her hand on his arm and arched her body up so that she was looking at him. 'It's worse.'

'Don't tell me that you're going to start spouting all that nonsense about mistakes.' As her full breasts pushed against his chest, Luc felt himself harden. He settled his hand on her juicy derrière and pulled her towards him so that their bodies were now so closely joined that a piece of paper couldn't have been slotted between them.

'I can't think straight when you're doing that.' Agatha expelled a long, shaky breath and her eyes fluttered. She slowly moved against his hard arousal. She couldn't get enough of him. Very lightly she touched his impressive erection and felt a heady sense of power as his big body shuddered against her.

'Ditto, you little witch.' Luc parted her legs with his hand and felt the slick moisture between them.

'Stop! We...we're having a conversation,' she panted,

ending on a moan of pure bliss as his questing finger found her sensitive spot and began gently teasing it.

When he slid into her and began grinding with beautiful, rhythmic movements, she lost complete track of their conversation, only dimly recalling it when he said with a sexy growl, 'I was going to say that, just in case you get it into your head to put this down to another oversight on both our parts, I'm just going to prove to you what we've got here is so damned good.' He flipped her so that she was on top of him, her luscious breasts dangling within reach of his mouth. He simultaneously suckled on one engorged nipple while she moved against him, building up to a tempo that had him struggling not to let go until she had reached her own splintering orgasm.

'So…' he murmured when she had finally surfaced. 'You were saying?' He kissed the tip of her nose and brushed her curly hair away from her face. She felt as though she was glued to him by a fine film of perspiration, and he liked that.

'I thought you were afraid that I might not be able to keep this…you know…? Under wraps,' Agatha ventured.

'It's a chance I'm willing to take.' Which was the closest he planned on getting to telling her that he trusted her—on that score, at least. She wasn't a gossip. Nor was he going to let her in on the weird, sick feeling he got when he thought of her doing something perfectly innocuous, like standing by a photocopier or bending over to stick some filing in a cabinet, while lecherous and quite probably married men sneaked covert glances at her fulsome assets.

'So when Helen returns?'

'You won't be going back to that cupboard.'

'I won't?'

'Remember that little publishing outfit you're so interested in?'

'You mean the one with the gardening books?'

'It'll need a little steering in the right direction. You have some good ideas.'

'You mean you actually listened to what I was saying?'

'So it would seem. You're going to take it over. You're not leaving my company. I want you where I can see you.'

'Are you just finding something for me to do?' Agatha asked the question tentatively. A little voice of reason pointed out that accepting a position for which she wasn't qualified smacked of an exchange of favours, but she swept aside that mental objection and focused on the thrilling prospect of continuing to work for him.

Alert to every nuance in her voice, Luc gave the smallest of shrugs. Then he said, with enough self-assurance to kill off any lingering doubt in her head, 'Don't underestimate yourself. You catch on quick. I'll set you up with a team of three to work out strategies for getting that publishing firm in the black. Management's been a bit unstable, and no one's bothered to drag it into the twenty-first century. They need to get on board with the fact that they can be undercut in price from any online bookstore. Personally, I don't have the time to devote to sorting them out. But you? You'd do a good job. I have every faith in you.'

Agatha could barely credit what she was hearing. Another subconscious tick was put in that box in her head. She snuggled against him, and within five minutes she was asleep.

Luc felt her relax against him and felt too her easy, regular breathing as she drifted off to sleep.

He had no idea why he had suggested what in fact was a truly meteoric promotion for someone with woefully inadequate qualifications but, having suggested it, he found that he was content with the prospect.

The publishing company was small and of relatively little value. There was a limit to how much damage she could inflict, although he really did have faith in her abilities. She had proved herself to be hard-working and talented, even if she did inherently dislike office work.

Warmed by the thought of having her around him whenever he wanted, and only vaguely aware that for the first time he had broken with tradition in allowing a woman to spend the night with him, Luc eventually fell asleep.

Five weeks later and Agatha was still on a high, still living on that fabulous cloud nine where hopes could truly blossom and the unthinkable might just come to pass.

She had been promoted without any fanfare in a move that had been shrewdly calculated to stifle any opportunity for wagging tongues to spread gossip. Much had been made of her gardening background, which was a unique talent in a company full of thrusting university graduates, and its relevance to the post she had been given.

Her little team of three had been recruited from outside and they had all been established in a cosy section of his building on the first floor. Agatha adored it. She had fellow gardening enthusiasts working with her and, whilst she wasn't physically working with plants, it was as close as she could possibly get from within the confines of an office.

Sometimes Luc would pop down to check their progress. He never gave any indication of having any interest in her aside from the purely professional, although Agatha was thrillingly aware of the lazy slant of his eyes in her direction, and the light brush of his fingers against her arm when he leaned over to inspect something on her computer.

Once, just once, they had both worked late, and when everyone else had vacated the building he had led her into his office and locked the door and they had made love right there with the low sofa as their bed and the desk as their foreplay arena.

He had confessed that it was the first time he had ever done that with any woman.

That, along with lots of other little things, was filed away in her head as 'significant'.

So far, her 'significant' box held a promising number of things, including his firsts: his first to have a woman stay the night with him—in fact to have practically moved in—his first to make love to a woman in his office, his first when it came to experiencing the delights of the local supermarket because he was accustomed to having his food delivered from Fortnum and Mason if he wasn't eating out. In fact, she reckoned that she might very well be the first woman he had entertained with a home-cooked meal, and afterwards a romantic comedy on the plasma television he swore they would never sit in front of.

All of that meant something. Agatha was sure of it.

Tonight, though, was going to be special. Luc would be heading off to New York for a week. She was going to leave work early and prepare something for him. Three courses, candlelight, wine, maybe even some mood music. She had already bought the ingredients for an Italian meal, and at precisely five o'clock she left, taking the tube and bus to her place, which seemed so much smaller and dingier in comparison than she could ever have imagined possible.

It was important to keep things real. That much she *did* know. He would be dropping by at a little after seven to take her to a mega-expensive restaurant on the outskirts of the city but she had cancelled the booking. Instead, they would eat in which was always so much cosier. The weather was nudging into Spring but it was still cold and rainy. By six thirty, she was dressed and when he buzzed her from downstairs she practically flew to the intercom to let him in.

Watching him as he divested himself of his trench coat and took in the candlelight and the carefully set table, she said breathlessly, 'I decided that it's better to stay in on the last night before you head off for your trip.' She was wearing a tight jade-green dress of a kind she would never have worn before, and nothing at all underneath it, which would previously have been unthinkable.

A trace of unease slivered through him. He hadn't expected her to cook for him, although thinking about it it was hardly the first time. He saw her most evenings and going out every night had not been feasible. He marvelled at how quickly she had infiltrated his life. Other women had been entertained on a sporadic basis, when it suited him. With Agatha he appeared to have developed a routine and he wasn't entirely sure when this had happened.

'There was no need,' he drawled, shifting his attention away from the table and the candles and on to her, which was a far less thought-provoking sight.

'I know, but I thought it would be nice for us to eat in. Honestly, I know it looks as though I've gone to a lot of trouble, but I really haven't. It's just a quick meal.'

Agatha tried to hide her disappointment at his less than enthusiastic response. But she felt awkward as she fussed around him, pouring him a glass of wine and laughing a little too brightly when he told her that candles were a fire hazard.

'Aren't you in the least bit romantic?' She tried very hard not to sound wistful, but Luc's shrewd green eyes still narrowed on her flushed, upturned face resting dreamily in the palm of one hand.

'No,' he told her abruptly, closing his knife and fork on a meal that he knew would have taken her quite a while to prepare. 'So let's not spoil the occasion by going down that road. Believe me—it leads to a dead end.' He pushed back his chair and watched her, his handsome face impassive.

Trapped in the suddenly uncomfortable silence, Agatha launched into a nervous explanation of what she had prepared for dessert. Luc relaxed. Hell, he wasn't going to be seeing her for a week, possibly longer if his meetings overran. There were better things to do than eat chocolate fondant. He smiled, tilting his head to one side.

'Let's skip the fondant,' he murmured, patting his lap and zeroing in on the sway of her magnificent body as she walked towards him. He eliminated his sense of foreboding with one decisive strike. 'I'm hungry for something else...'

'You only ever think about sex,' Agatha half-laughed, although she could hear the thread of seriousness in her voice. But she sighed and yielded to her very passionate lover as he gently eased the stretchy dress off her shoulders, groaning with appreciation at the sight of her bare breasts.

He could do this to her, make all her thought processes come to a grinding halt just with one touch.

When he delicately lifted one heavy breast to his mouth, she wriggled on his lap and succumbed utterly to the soaring pleasure rushing through her like an unstoppable tide.

Somewhere along the line, he growled that this would be the last time he made love to her in her bedsit, because it was just too damned uncomfortable; she heard herself purr contentedly because that suited her fine.

Her bed might have been a lot smaller than his, but he still managed to touch her in all the right places, unerringly finding the pulsing heat of her womanhood and stoking it until she was whimpering to be brought to a climax.

He never tired of hearing that husky catch in her voice when she begged for him, and he never tired of the sight of her stripped bare with her fair hair in tousled curls around her face and her creamy, smooth, voluptuous body writhing on the bed, caught up in the mindless pleasure only he could arouse in her.

Even though he knew that she was his, possession had not yet dimmed his craving for her. Sometimes at work he would find himself propelled down to her floor on the pretext of asking her something for no better reason than he wanted the pleasure of the accidental touch.

Knowing that he would not be with her for a while, he wanted to make their love-making last. Time and again he teased her, stroking her with his fingers, his mouth, his tongue, until she was lost. When he did finally thrust into her, she was wet and hot for him and it was an earth-shattering experience.

Still tender from their extended love-making, Agatha curled against him and half-closed her eyes when he ran his fingers through her hair.

'Are you going to miss me?' She eventually sighed, and Luc stilled, because there was an undercurrent to that question that was as loud to him as the clanging of church bells.

Which seemed an unfortunate allusion.

'I'm going to be as busy as hell.' He refused to be pinned down and he felt her shift against him, propping herself up and looking at him evenly.

'What does that mean?'

'It means I probably won't have time to think about anything apart from making sure that we get this deal done.'

A chill breeze seemed to feather its way along her spine. She knew that she should just steer away from the topic, but perversely she couldn't.

'Will you call me?'

'What's going on here? What's this all about?'

Two things were becoming blindingly clear to Agatha.

The first was that he couldn't commit to calling her, and the second was that he couldn't commit to calling her because he wasn't even going to notice her absence. Maybe the absence of sex with her, but not *her*.

She had dressed up what they had in lots of frills and bows and called it a relationship that was really going somewhere, but the truth was that it was all about the sex for Luc. Good heavens, he couldn't even enjoy the dessert she had spent an hour and a half making the afternoon before, because he had wanted to get into bed with her.

Shame and anger curdled into a heady mix. She pulled away from him and sat up, arms folded, staring blindly ahead of her.

'You tell me,' Agatha said quietly. 'I don't know how it happened, but we're lovers.'

'You *don't know how it happened*? It happened because we can't resist one another.' He pulled her against him but she resisted and Luc, sitting up now as well, threw his hands up in a gesture that was both elegant and telling.

'Okay. What do you want me to say? That I'll call you? I'll call you.' He was infuriated that she had contrived to spoil their last evening together for what might well run into two weeks by demanding answers from him that he wasn't prepared to provide. He wasn't a man who enjoyed being penned into a corner. Frankly, any such manoeuvre from a woman was charged with risk. But he would make the concession. Why not? He wanted her more than he had wanted any woman for a very long time. She did wonders for his jaded palate, and for that reason he would relinquish his natural urge to slam his instinctive barriers into place.

'Now can we move on?' he asked, trailing his finger along the tiny ridges of her spine and then smiling as he watched the tiny responsive flex of her body. Her mouth might be saying one thing but her body was singing a completely different song, and the body could be very persuasive indeed. 'I'll phone you every day if you want,' he volunteered magnanimously.

'I don't want you to phone me!' Her eyes felt blurry now and she shrugged off his hand. She was rigid with tension. Like a high-wire walker who had taken the first step over the abyss, she now felt committed to carry on, no turning back. 'I don't want you to phone me because I've kicked up a fuss,' she told him, her face half-inclined in his direction. 'How desperate do you think I am?'

'I never said anything about you being desperate,' Luc groaned and muttered an oath of sheer frustration under his breath.

'But it's what you're thinking. And I don't blame you. I fell into bed with you and I've accommodated you every inch of the way!'

'You're getting hysterical.'

'I am not getting hysterical!' But she took a few deep breaths. 'I just...I just want to know where this is going.'

'Why is it important? We're having fun, aren't we?'

'There's more to life than having fun.'

Luc drew in a long, even breath. 'I don't want to get involved in this conversation. What we have is good. Why question it?'

'Because I need to know if I'm wasting my time with you.'

Luc's experience with women had not braced him for such a direct line of questioning. In the past, women had tried to infiltrate themselves into his life. They had never pinned him to the spot and demanded to know what his intentions were. They had nurtured implausible expectations which had manifested themselves in a sudden interest in the decor of his apartment, or a pressing need to prove what good cooks they were. Inevitably, that had signalled the end. Never had any of them come right out and asked him if they were wasting their time. What kind of a question was that?

For a few seconds, he was literally speechless.

'I'm going to have a shower,' he hedged, getting out of bed. Agatha scrambled behind him, grabbing one of her oversized tee-shirts en route.

'That's not an answer!' She screeched to a halt as he turned on the shower and stepped under it. He dwarfed the miniscule shower cubicle. Within seconds the bathroom was all steamed up. She took a few seconds to think about what she was going to say while she watched him with that compulsive fascination that she had always known to be a sign of weakness. She loved this man. She had let herself fall deeper and deeper in love with him while he had steadfastly stuck to the programme and enjoyed her for sex. In no way could she say that he had ever led her up a garden path.

'I thought I could do this,' Agatha managed to get out when the shower had been switched off and she wasn't having to shout above the sound of running water. 'I thought I could be a thoroughly modern person and have an affair with you because I'm attracted to you, but I can't.' She looked down at her fingers because it felt safer than to stare at him.

For a while, Luc didn't say anything. He began putting on his clothes. He didn't know why he should feel as if a rocket had exploded underneath him. Hadn't he known all along that she was the old-fashioned sort of girl who engaged in relationships in the hope that they were going somewhere? He wondered how he could have ignored that simple, central truth and allowed his actions to be ruled by the driving power of lust. But he had, and he was repelled by his own weakness.

'I'm sorry to hear that.' He addressed her downbent head, steeling himself against the insidious pull of sexual attraction which had been his downfall in the first place. 'And I wish I could let you buy into the fantasy that this will end in a walk up an aisle somewhere, but I can't.' He raked his fingers through his still-damp hair and frowned. 'Look at me when I'm talking to you. Please.'

Agatha reluctantly looked at him, although she strongly wanted to cover her ears and not hear what he was going to say.

'I don't know where this is going to end, or when, but marriage is never going to be on the cards.'

'You can't stay a bachelor all your life.' There. It was out in the open.

'When and if I ever do decide to get married,' Luc delivered grimly, 'It will be to a woman who understands my priorities. I've never told anyone this, but I'm going to tell you now because you deserve honesty: I was involved with a woman when my father died and I was summoned home.' His mouth twisted in distaste at the memory. 'I was faced with a mess that needed clearing up, and the only way I could clear it up was to jump in at the deep end. I worked twenty-four-hour days, seven days a week. Needless to say,' he said with biting sarcasm, 'The love of my life didn't understand having to take a back seat to work commitments that were unavoidable. So, Agatha, I don't do the romantic dramas. Not now, not ever.'

What he didn't add was that he would eventually settle down with someone whose drive and ambition matched his own, or who was content to allow him the freedom to continue with life exactly as he wanted. He didn't want the shrew in the background nagging away at him, telling him that he needed to work less, rolling her eyes to the ceiling every time he had to go abroad, trying to turn him into a domesticated, obedient man about the house. It was a well-rehearsed piece of wisdom he had lived by for as long as he could remember. He wondered why it now sounded like a tired cliché.

'I know you haven't got a clue what I'm talking about, but believe me you'll thank me for being honest with you one day. I'm not the sort of guy you need.'

'No, you're not,' Agatha said bitterly.

'You're looking for someone who wants to join you with his head in the clouds and that person is never going to be me.'

'Did you ever care about me at all?' The question was torn out of her. She set her mouth in a stubborn line and looked at him.

'Of course I cared about you.' But his voice was rife with discomfort.

'You mean you cared about sleeping with me. Maybe I was a complete idiot to think that we could be a significant part of each other's lives. I just can't believe that I've spent all this time, *wasted* all this time, falling in love with you!' Agatha blinked rapidly to clear her vision, which was going a little misty.

'I never asked you to,' Luc told her, a dark flush accentuating the dramatic contours of his face. He squashed the treacherous streak of satisfaction her admission generated in him under the ruthless onward march of pure, cool logic.

A woman in love was a responsibility. However great the sex was, he could not and would not encourage her to nurture pointless dreams.

Agatha hung her head.

'I could pretend that this was what you want, but I won't, because I'm not that bloody minded.' Her continuing silence, rather than hastening his departure, seemed to root him to the spot. 'When...when did you realise that you were in love with me?' On cue, his body reacted and he turned away abruptly.

'I don't want to talk about it.'

'No. Understandable.'

'I didn't want to. I *knew* that you weren't the kind of guy who did commitment. But I started hoping…'

Luc was mesmerised by the lone tear that trickled down her cheek and plopped onto her fingers. He extracted a wad of tissues from the box on the chest of drawers and shoved them into her hand.

'I should have done that Internet thing. It might have led somewhere.'

Luc didn't want to get into a conversation about the dangers of Internet dating. Even knowing that she was already slipping into history, he still didn't want to think of her sleeping with anyone else.

Agatha heard everything his silence was telling her. Yes, she should have done the Internet thing. They had had their fun, but she had a nesting instinct he was incapable of fulfilling. She cringed when she thought of how uncomfortable he must be, standing there while she wept and poured her heart out. It was just the sort of emotional weakness guaranteed to get on his nerves, but she wasn't able to help herself.

'It's regrettable that things have turned out this way.' Luc dragged his attention away from her and focused on bringing things back down to a level he could understand. 'But I think it's important that we get one thing straight: in no way will this impact on your job, so I don't want you handing in your resignation.'

Her fair hair tumbled over her shoulders and he could just about make out the cartoon logo on the front of the tee-shirt she had dragged on. He cleared his throat and shoved his hands into his pockets. 'You and your team are autonomous and I will ensure that Jefferies take over immediate supervision. I fully appreciate that, feeling the way you do, it might be difficult having to report directly to me.'

Agatha nodded. She felt she could hear the gentle pity in his voice, but how could she possibly get angry when she had provided him with just cause to feel like that? She took a deep, shaky breath and finally looked up at him.

'Thank you,' she said stiffly. 'I appreciate that. I'm really enjoying this project and I think I can make a real go of it.' She tore the tissue paper into little strips and then continued playing with it, giving her hands something to do and her eyes something to focus on.

'I don't know how it happened, but I let things go too far.' He couldn't free himself from the savage urge to explain himself to her.

'I'm not Miranda.'

'How do you know her name?'

'I just do. I know she must have hurt you dreadfully, but...' *But what?* She hated herself for continuing to cling.

'She taught me a valuable lesson.'

'She taught you how to become an island.'

Okay, so there was some truth in that statement, Luc recognized. But what was wrong with being an island? It was a damned sight safer to be self-reliant. But something deep inside jarred painfully, like shards of glass scraping through his flesh, and it was too heroic an effort to squash the feeling and to grope his way back to common sense.

Common sense prevailed. He was off-balance because, not only had Agatha laid her cards on the table with a forthrightness that would have had any man struggling to regroup, but in addition she looked strained, and that was all the more noticeable because he had only seen her laughing and relaxed around him for the past few weeks.

He had become accustomed to her. Of course there would be some guilt involved in causing her suffering. That was what had him feeling so sick to the stomach.

'It's because I care about you that I'm walking away, and

you would be smart to trust my experience here. I can't give you the love you want.' Every word tasted of poison. Had he felt this way with Miranda when the end had finally come? He couldn't remember. It had been a turning point in his life so *why* couldn't he remember? 'I'm going to go now. Is there anyone you could call up to stay with you?'

Agatha glared at him with undisguised hostility. That, she thought, was really taking the whole pity angle too far!

'I'm breaking off our relationship, Luc—or whatever you want to call it—because I know you don't *do* relationships. It's not the end of the world. These things happen and I'll be a stronger person for it. So, no, I don't *need* to call up anyone to stay with me. I may have been a complete fool but I'm actually not as pathetic as you think I am.' She was determined to cling to whatever shreds of dignity she had left. She didn't blame him for how things had turned out, she blamed herself, and she would pick herself up bit by bit if it killed her in the process.

'And, yes, I *would* appreciate it if you didn't pop down to where I happen to be working if you can help it—although, if you have to, it won't be the end of the world and I won't need someone close by to prop me up in case I get a fit of the vapours.' It had taken everything she possessed to say those words but at least he wasn't looking at her with that horrible, patronising sympathy she had spotted earlier. She had given him the excuse he needed to drop the condolences on her stupidity, and the accompanying pep talk on how to survive him, and there was a guarded expression on his face now.

She drew in a deep breath. Recovery had to start some-where, and she could deal with 'guarded' a lot better than she could deal with pity.

CHAPTER SEVEN

Luc looked across the table to the striking redhead who had smiled coquettishly at him for the duration of the meal, undeterred by his unimpressive range of responses to her forays into conversation. He knew that he could sit there and display all the communication skills of a brick and she would still continue smiling and flirting; free, single and unattached, he was the most eligible guy in town.

Right now, they were winding up an eye-wateringly expensive meal at one of the top restaurants in London. It was game on to return to his apartment, where she would let him have all the assets that had been so conspicuously on display for the course of the very long and very tedious evening.

It wasn't going to happen. For the past three weeks his libido had been alarmingly unobliging. In fact, it had been non-existent. This was the first time he had actually felt driven to make an effort and he should have been enjoying the well-rehearsed game that would inevitably lead to the bedroom.

Instead, he had looked at his watch five times and was politely now waiting for her to finish her coffee so that he could get the bill and head back to his place. Alone. He had planned his excuse five minutes into their date.

The whole situation was enough to set his teeth on edge, from his lack of interest in the opposite sex to his continuing preoccupation with a woman who should have been halfway to being forgotten. She had known from the very start that he just wasn't the kind of guy who hurtled towards commitment like a kamikaze pilot hell-bent on self-destruction. He had his rules and she had chosen not to play by them at the end of the day.

He should have been breathing a sigh of profound relief at his narrow escape. He was not interested or, for that matter, ready for commitment to anyone. When that time did arrive, it wouldn't be with someone like Agatha who would expect a fairy tale, with bows and ribbons and a cherry on top.

Instead, she had been playing on his mind with the aggravating persistence of some distant song he just couldn't quite seem to get out of his head.

Not even the failsafe solution of work had come to the rescue. He had been putting in all the hours God made; indeed, he had been out of the country more often than he had been in it. But he had not been able to avoid infuriating lapses of concentration during which he would catch himself frowning off into the distance while the rest of the world disappeared into temporary oblivion.

And now this. Five foot eleven inches of obliging, drop-dead gorgeousness and he couldn't care less. He could have spent the last three hours sitting opposite a troll.

'Are you listening to me?' Annabel leant forward so that he could all but see the nipples peeping above the low-cut neckline of her dress. Poker-straight hair framed a face that could stop traffic.

'No, not really.' He signalled for the bill and felt a twinge of pity for the faltering smile that greeted this slice of unadorned truth. Agatha would disapprove of this level of brutal honesty. 'I've got a heck of a lot on my mind at the moment with work.' He shrugged and raised both hands in a gesture of eloquent regret. 'Bad time to be asking a woman

CATHY WILLIAMS 121

out.' He was vaguely surprised to be going into so much lengthy detail. 'You're a very attractive woman, Annabel, but I'm not in the running for any kind of relationship at the moment.'

'Work?' That was her way out of an embarrassing situation, and the single word hovered in the air between them until he nodded.

'My feet are hardly going to touch ground for the next few months and a girl like you deserves a guy who can do her justice.' He settled the bill, barely registering the outrageous amount.

'You don't know what you're missing.' Annabel stood up, rescuing her turquoise, bejewelled clutch-bag from the table. 'But thank you for being honest with me from the beginning. It probably wouldn't have worked anyway,' she added, slipping a shawl around her shoulders. 'I like my men to be a little less stodgy.'

Stodgy? As Eddy drove him back to his apartment, Luc couldn't help but think that that description might very well have been the highlight of the evening. It was the only time he had felt the inclination to laugh out loud, at any rate.

His road was quiet by the time they pulled into a parking space and the building that housed his penthouse apartment even more so. He let himself in, took the stairs instead of the lift, silently let himself into the apartment and was heading towards the kitchen for a whisky nightcap when the sound of her voice stopped him dead in his tracks.

For a few seconds, Luc had the weirdest feeling that he had become the victim of his own inconvenient imagination. He turned round very slowly and noticed her perched at the end of the sofa, staring up at him with those enormous blue eyes. He should have seen her the minute he entered, because she had switched on the light by the sofa and was making no effort to conceal herself, but his mind had been a million miles away.

'I'm…I'm sorry. I let myself in. I was going to wait outside. In fact, I did wait outside, but it started getting chilly and it's so quiet around here. I got a little spooked. I, um, used the spare key you gave me. I forgot to give it back to you when we, um…' Agatha ran out of words and just looked at him. True to his word, he hadn't stepped foot in her office since they had broken up. All her dealings had been with one of his henchmen. In fact, he hadn't been in the country at all, or at least not much. She had found out that much from asking around, even though she had known how silly it was to maintain even that slim thread of interest in his movements.

Now, starved of the sight of him for three weeks, she guiltily drank him in like an addict caving in to just one more hit.

'What are you doing here? Why the hell didn't you return the key to me when you found out that you still had it?'

Tension ratcheted up in Luc, but alongside that there lurked a perverse feeling of satisfaction, because there could be only one reason she would have dumped all her lofty principles and returned to his apartment. She might have wafted lyrical about love and marriage and the 'happy ever after', but three weeks on and she couldn't do without him or the passion she had been so quick to dismiss. She had underestimated the power of lust and that came as no surprise to him. Nor did the fact that she hadn't returned the key to his front door. Psychologically, she would have held on to it as a telling reminder of what she needed whether she wanted to admit it or not.

'I forgot, I guess.'

'In that case, you can hand it over now.' He looked at his watch and then stared down at her with a cool, shuttered expression. 'You've effectively broken into my apartment. Now that you're here, I can't throw you out onto the streets, but in case you hadn't noticed you and I are old news. In fact, you should consider yourself lucky that I have work to do tonight, otherwise I wouldn't have returned alone.'

Agatha's face turned a shade of mortified pink. Out of the loop, she hadn't heard a word about Luc's extra-curricular activities, nor had she glimpsed any headlines in the gossip columns which she had devoured with shameful enthusiasm. Her mind began to stray and she firmly clamped it back into place because this was not the time.

Nerves were tearing through her, sharp teeth that were making a nonsense of any semblance of calm she was trying to project. It didn't help that he was standing there, looking at her as though she was something noxious that had crawled out from under a bush.

Luc had moved on big time. Was she surprised? No. Like commitment, standing still was something he didn't do. He wasn't someone given to pining or even reflection when it came to the women he left behind.

Was she hurt? Desperately. But she took a deep breath and tried not to focus on that.

It had taken a lot to come here.

'Oh. Yes. Right.' She wondered whether he had reverted to his leggy blondes. Had she been the exception to the rule? 'I wanted to tell you this face to face.'

'I really can't believe that you have anything to say to me of a personal nature, and anything else can be discussed in my office.' He turned his back to her and strolled into the open-plan kitchen for the glass of whisky he had promised himself. More than ever, he figured he needed one, although it had to be said that the evening had acquired a certain *patina* that had snapped him out of his edgy, discontented mood.

Agatha sighed and half-rose from the chair, only to fall back into it. He couldn't have made it any clearer that he wanted her out of his apartment. Did he think that if she got too close she might stage a surprise attack and fling a ball and chain around his neck before he could escape?

The enormity of what she was doing there hit her like a brick and she swallowed painfully, watching him as he poured himself a drink. It *would* be whisky. It was the only nightcap he allowed himself, and then only occasionally. He might need more than one tonight.

'So…?' Luc turned around, every muscle in his body totally relaxed as he propped himself up against the granite counter that partially separated the kitchen from the open living-area. 'Say your piece.' He swirled the ice round in his glass and took a deep mouthful as he continued to watch her intently above the rim of the glass. She looked as nervous as a kitten. Nervous and vulnerable.

The silence lengthened between them until he finally clicked his tongue impatiently and strode towards where she was huddled on the sofa. She couldn't have been more different from his date earlier on, who had been the epitome of cool, impeccably groomed, self-assured elegance.

Not the kind of woman who would cling to fantasies of picket fences, rosy-cheeked children and a domesticated husband who couldn't wait to race back to hearth and home. He hung onto this thought because, even looking like a lost waif and stray, Agatha was still managing to exert a crazy sexual pull that he could do without.

'Is it about money?' he demanded, which brought her head up in surprise. 'Because, if it is, then you've got it.'

'What are you going on about?'

'You've come here out of the blue,' Luc informed her caustically. 'And I doubt it's because you suddenly decided on paying me a social visit to discuss old times.' He felt his eyes drift over her and on cue he imagined her naked underneath the cover-all jacket and baggy clothes. The rebelliousness of his mind made him grit his teeth in rage and frustration.

'But I wasn't born yesterday and my knowledge of women is extensive.' He poured the remainder of his drink down his throat and flung himself on the chrome-and-leather sofa, facing her. 'We went out—maybe you got to thinking that you really exited the situation before you could retrieve any material benefits.'

Luc shrugged as though his conclusions, cynical though they might be, were to be expected. 'I don't have to remind you that you happen to be in an incredibly well-paid job which was tailor-made for you, but I suppose you *have* seen first-hand how my women are treated when I'm finished with them. Maybe you've decided that you deserve your own golden handshake? After all, you *did* enjoy privileges beyond the norm.' He glanced around him. Keys to his apartment, for one thing. And then a level of normalcy that, thinking about it now, was really fairly astounding. He chose not to dwell on that.

Agatha, leaning forward with her hands clasped on her knees, couldn't believe what she was hearing. Her mouth had dropped open.

'I have no problem with that,' Luc informed her magnanimously. 'Fair's fair, after all, and you *do* need to move out of that dump.'

'I *have* moved out!' Agatha dealt with that particular misconception straightaway.

'When?' Evidence of an independence he didn't know she had made him flush darkly. Okay, he didn't like it.

'It doesn't matter. A week and a half ago. I found somewhere a bit closer to work in a nicer area.'

'Another bedsit with a crazy landlord who thinks that

mould on the walls constitutes the equivalent of patterned wallpaper?'

'No. I can afford a proper flat.' Which brought her mind swinging back to his accusations of wanting his money. 'Thanks to my generous salary. And I'm not here to try and talk you into giving me money. How could you think that I would be the sort of person to do that?'

'Most women are motivated by money.'

'I'm not *most women*, and I'm really hurt that you can sling me into that category as if…as if you don't know me at all.'

Luc scowled, on the back foot now as she looked at him with huge, hurt, accusing eyes.

'Okay.' He held both hands up in a gesture of defeat. 'So you haven't come here on a begging mission. Why, then?'

'I won't beat about the bush here, Luc. I know you're a great believer in getting straight to the point: I'm pregnant.'

For a few seconds, Luc had the strange sensation that time had slowed to a standstill and his brain was trying to function in a pool of treacle. He wondered if he had heard correctly. 'That's impossible,' he said at last, but he couldn't keep still. He stood up and began prowling through the room, raking his fingers through his hair, finally halting in front of her with narrowed eyes. 'You told me you were on the pill. I trusted you. Were you lying?' Then, as if those questions were already giving too much credence to the unthinkable, he repeated, forcefully, 'You can't be.'

'I did four tests, Luc.' She reached into her bag with a wildly beating heart and extracted a small plastic bag in which a little piece of cream plastic with two bright blue lines glared back at him triumphantly.

'This can't be happening.' He sat down heavily and regarded her with such disbelieving intensity that every syllable of the speech she had rehearsed flew out of her head with the speed of an army of rats deserting a sinking ship.

'I know it's a shock; it was a shock to me too.' She had been getting backache and had eventually gone to see her local doctor. She had expected to emerge from the surgery with a prescription for some strong painkillers and maybe some advice to get a massage. Instead, she had left on wobbly legs, having been told that she was just over two months' pregnant.

'I *was* on the pill,' she explained in a shaky undertone. 'But not that first time. That first time, we made love without any contraception. I didn't think anything would happen.'

'You *didn't think…*' Luc shook his head as reality nudged past his dazed disbelief and claimed its rightful place. Life as he knew it was about to change because she *hadn't thought*, although he had to share the responsibility for that as well. He should have taken precautions himself. He always had. But not with her. Things had happened fast and furious and he hadn't stopped to consider the consequences.

'I'm sorry.' Agatha tried to find some strength from the fact that he wasn't punching anything. She herself had had over a day to think about the situation and to try and come to terms with it. He, on the other hand, had not. How hard would it be for him now, fresh back home from a hot date, to discover that he was going to be a daddy in under seven months' time by a woman he no longer wanted in his life?

'You said there was no chance. I remember; you said it had been safe.'

His life was still in the process of crashing and burning.

'I really thought I was. I promised that I wouldn't stay long here, Luc. I wasn't sure whether I should tell you or not, but of course I knew that I had to. Look, perhaps I should go now. Leave you to try and come to terms with it.' She made a move to stand up and he ordered her to sit back down.

'And then what?' He stared at her, his normally vibrantly, bronzed skin ashen.

'I haven't come here to ask for anything. I just thought that you had to know. I don't expect you to change your life in any way.'

'Are you crazy? How can my life not change?'

'I don't need looking after, Luc. I'm more than capable and happy to be a single mother.'

'This coming from the girl who had dreams of love and marriage?'

'Let's just say that I've grown up.'

'And I'm supposed to do what, exactly? Fill me in here on this life of mine that's not going to change.'

'You carry on working, going out with women, and when the baby's born we can start talking about visiting rights. If, that is, you want to visit.'

'Are you on the same planet as me, Agatha?'

'I'm trying to make this easy for you.'

'You must fancy your chances as a magician if you think you've succeeded in doing that. What, for instance, do you intend to tell your mother? Do you think she'll fall for the stork scenario?'

'I, well, I haven't actually crossed that bridge just yet. I'm only just getting used to the idea myself, and Mum…she's old-fashioned. I can't face the thought of breaking this to her right now. I have to find some courage from somewhere first.'

'Then I suggest you do. I also suggest you don't try and stonewall by refusing to tell her who the father is. I can't take back what's happened, but I assure you that I intend to take full responsibility for any child of mine. I'm not interested in secrecy.'

'What do you mean by *full responsibility*?'

'You will be looked after financially. So will the child.' His eyes flitted to her stomach. *His child!* Not in a million years could he have ever foreseen his life becoming so spectacularly derailed, but he had to concede that there was something very sexy about the fact that she was carrying his baby in her stomach. 'Where have you moved?' He reluctantly dragged glittering eyes away from her stomach. 'Your idea of appropriate accommodation doesn't coincide with mine.'

'You can't just *take over*!'

'I'm the other half of this equation. I have as much say where you live when you're pregnant with my baby. Which brings us to the fundamental question of our relationship.'

'We don't *have* a relationship.' Suddenly everything seemed to be moving at breakneck speed.

'Like it or not, we do now, and something in me's telling me that your cherished dream might be about to come true.'

Agatha didn't have to ask for clarification on that statement. She knew exactly what he was talking about, in that wry, bitter voice. They had ended their brief affair on her outburst about wanting more than just a temporary liaison. Now, against his will, he had somehow been driven into a corner by a situation he hadn't courted and wouldn't have wanted in a million years. She had told him that his life would remain unchanged. How could she have believed that? He wasn't the sort of man who ducked responsibility, even a responsibility he didn't want.

'I won't marry you,' she whispered. 'That's not why I came here. That's not why I've told you that I'm pregnant.'

'You must know that I wouldn't be prepared to stand on the sidelines, and you must also know that no child of mine will be illegitimate. I have honour, Agatha. If you're so willing to remind me that I *must* know you, and therefore *must* know that you would never be the sort of woman to engineer a situation like this for her own benefit, then *you* must surely know *me* as well—or at least know me well enough to realise that I'm not the sort of man who would fling money at the problem and then walk away.'

'I don't care whether you're prepared to stand on the sidelines or not. I know you think that I'm a hopeless romantic who believes in stuff that you don't, but that doesn't mean that I'm a hopeless human being. A hopeless human being would...' In her head a single word reverberated like a gunshot: *problem*. Luc had been presented with a problem and he was dealing with it with the cold-blooded efficiency with which he dealt with all the problems he encountered in his life—the only difference being that this particular problem was growing inside her.

Luc jumped into the faltering silence. 'A hopeless human being would...what? Put her child before herself? Provide a stable environment? Do the right thing?'

'That's not what we're talking about,' Agatha muttered in a shaken voice.

'No? Then explain. We will be married, because it's the only possible solution to the dilemma.'

'It's not a *dilemma* and it's not a *problem*.'

'Okay. What would you like to call it? Situation? Unexpected chance event? Fateful occurrence? Choose your description. It makes little difference to the solution.'

'I'm really tired, Luc.' Agatha stood up, suddenly drained by the crazy onslaught of emotions attacking her from every angle. The ground that should have felt steady under her feet began to sway. It was like being on a boat in the middle of a choppy ocean, complete with feelings of nausea and giddiness.

'And I don't feel very well. The doctor told me that I'm

anaemic.' Her eyelids fluttered and she was dimly aware of being caught in mid-fall and swept off her feet while she struggled to contain her sickness.

In the very split second that her face had gone from its argumentative pink colour to chalk-white, Luc had been galvanized into action, catching her before she had time to collapse in a heap on the ground.

Barely had he had time to get his head around the life-changing bombshell that had been thrown at his feet like a careless hand grenade than he was racked with guilt at having dealt with the situation in a heavy-handed manner. Heavy handed, he belatedly recognised, might work for most things but it wasn't going to work here. He had reduced her to a fainting fit, and in her condition it was the very last thing she needed.

He carried her into his bedroom and gently laid her on the bed, propping her up on the soft pillows as she gradually blinked back to reality.

'Did I faint?' she whispered, reaching out and holding onto the collar of his shirt with one small hand. She felt vulnerable, fragile and scared and she just couldn't bear the thought of him leaving the room. Much as she hated it, she felt anchored by his very solid presence.

'Yes. Is it the first time it's happened?'

Agatha nodded mutely.

'You haven't been eating. Shouldn't you be bigger by now? You're as light as a feather. '

'Why are you fussing?' Agatha pursued doggedly. 'You don't care about…about this. It's just something that's come along to disrupt your life. You like to be in control of everything, and this is the one thing you can't control even if you think you can.' Her eyes filled up and she looked down hurriedly, willing them away.

'I'm calling a doctor,' Luc told her in such a gentle voice

that she had to try even harder not to cry. In full vent, Luc could be cold and intimidating and send her shooting off into realms of anger she'd hardly known she possessed. He could also be thoughtful and touchingly humane in equal measure. How had she forgotten that?

He ignored her feeble, automatic protest and half-turned away to make the call, then he spun back round to face her, sitting on the side of the bed and leaning on one hand.

'I didn't know you could get a doctor to make a visit just like that. Not that it's necessary.'

'It is necessary,' Luc informed her. 'And I have a hotline to the best doctor in London.'

'Because you're ill all the time?' She was beginning to feel sleepy and she yawned and wriggled on the bed, surprised that she could even consider nodding off when she was full of so much unresolved, pent-up emotion. She realised that she was still clutching at his shirt and she slowly released her grip.

'I'm not going to marry you,' she told him, just in case.

'I'm not going to fight with you again. You need to look after yourself and waging war with me isn't going to help.'

'I'm not waging war.'

'There you go again.'

The softness in his voice made her want to smile. She was still feeling stupidly content when the doorbell rang and a middle-aged, grey-haired man with a gentle face and shrewd, black eyes was ushered into the bedroom. While he took her pulse and examined her, he told her that he had known the family for years on a personal level, and had been Luc's doctor since Luc had moved to London to live.

'Not that I see very much of him,' he said, packing away his black bag and moving to the door where Luc had been impatiently waiting, having been dispatched there by an adamant Agatha.

'So? What's the prognosis, Roberto?' Luc frowned at Agatha who still looked incredibly wan.

'You need rest, my dear,' Roberto said, turning to face Agatha, his lined face serious. 'Your blood pressure's up, which could lead to all sorts of problems if it doesn't settle, and whilst the baby's heartbeat is strong enough I don't like those shadows under your eyes. You're obviously stressed and probably not taking in the nutrients that you should. Of course, there is no reason to eat for two, my dear, but you do need certain vital minerals so you need to eat well. I'm going to give you a prescription for folic acid, but more importantly I'm going to insist that you rest. At least for the next month until things settle. And that's an order!'

He smiled when he said that. Not that Agatha felt equipped to return the smile. How was it possible that she could have travelled such an enormous distance in such a compacted space of time? From utter confusion and panic to a complete inability to deal with the possible loss of the tiny, growing baby inside her that had generated the panic in the first place.

A range of frightening possibilities buzzed in her fraught brain as she watched Luc usher the doctor out of the room, talking to him rapidly in a low voice.

When he returned a few minutes later, his face was implacable, and Agatha felt a knot of fear twist in her stomach.

'He was lying, wasn't he?' she whispered. 'He was lying to be kind, but really it's much more serious than he told me. I know it. I can see it on your face.'

'Really? Then we need to do something about getting your eyes tested.' He resumed his place sitting on the bed next to her.

Three weeks without her had been hellishly long. Whilst he had in no way anticipated that the chain of events between them could possibly have led to this moment in time, he was fully resolved on what he needed to do.

And, first off the bat, getting her in a lather by trying to impose his will on her was out of the question.

Under no condition, he had been told by Roberto, was she to be unduly stressed. So trying to bludgeon her into marriage because it satisfied his sense of honour was going to have to go on the back burner. But look after her he would, because the idea of having a baby with her had grown on him with astonishing ease. Maybe, he had thought as Roberto had chatted to him, because the presence of the doctor had somehow turned the abstract into the real. At any rate, he would now approach his mission to protect her with all the military efficiency at his disposal, whether she liked it or not. And no one could say that he didn't have bags of it.

'I may have said things that upset you,' he began in a conciliatory voice. 'And for that accept my apologies.'

'Pardon?'

'Don't push it.' Luc smiled crookedly and was aware of her relaxing with a sense of keen satisfaction. 'I'm no good at apologies, as a rule.'

'No,' Agatha agreed distractedly, fascinated by a Luc temporarily shorn of his bold arrogance. 'I guess you don't get enough practice.'

'No need. I'm usually right.' Why understate the truth?

It was a remark so typical of him that Agatha felt her lips twitch in amusement. Lord, but she had missed him. Had missed the look of him, the sound of him, the feel of him and the glorious touch of him, and having him sitting next to her on his bed was enough to make her want to swoon.

'I won't beat about the bush. Roberto says you need rest. So as of now you are on indefinite leave from your job.' He held up his hand to silence the protest he could see rising to her lips. 'There's no argument here, Agatha. You carry on working and you jeopardise the baby. Simple as that.'

Already his mind was working and coming up with a plan of action and it was a good feeling. 'Are you prepared for that?' he asked, and nodded slightly as she shook her head. 'Didn't think so. I'm also guessing that you might not be too keen on going back to the family fold just yet.'

'You know Mum.' Agatha stared off worriedly into the distance and chewed her lip. 'I…just need a bit of time. I only just found out,' she spluttered and was brought back down to reality when he took her hand in his. The physical touch, reassuring and unthreatening, sent a flood of heated awareness rushing through her, which was silly when he was just being nice.

'Understood. And, while we're on the subject of all things family, let me just tell you that I was totally out of order when it came to dealing with this…' Luc almost fell into the trap of calling it a 'situation' once again '…unexpected occurrence. I reacted like a caveman. Sure, family honour is important, but I'm willing to concede that we no longer live in the Dark Ages. So let's forget about that proposal of mine and just focus on getting you fighting fit.'

Never had he been more placatory with a member of the opposite sex. But, then again, never had he been in a position of very nearly causing untold damage because of his own crass behaviour. He had learnt a valuable lesson and he wasn't about to disregard it. He might not have wasted a second thinking about settling down, but he was in a place without option, if only she was aware of it. Agatha, as a single mother, would set about looking for her dream guy with intent. Hadn't she already considered the Internet in her search? And there was no way that Luc was going to have his own flesh and blood brought up by another man.

But he had effectively ruled himself out of the running

by turning her down flat when she had looked at him with those big, dewy eyes and started talking about romance and fairy-tale marriages. He had hurt her and his mission now was to regain her trust.

'Fighting fit?' Agatha was beginning to feel a little dazed by his sudden *volte face*. His rapid backtracking from the crazy marriage proposal was a blessing, she told herself. But it still hurt that he had obviously had a light-bulb moment and had realised that, however high the honour stakes were, settling down with a woman for whom he felt nothing beyond maybe some affection and a keen sense of duty was just ridiculous. As he had said, his perfect woman didn't come attached to a bunch of emotional strings. She could feel herself getting breathless and worked up all over again and swallowed it back.

'You need to rest,' Luc informed her. 'And London is no place for resting. I have a house in a very quiet, rural area in Berkshire. It's close enough to London to commute but far away enough to forget what noise pollution sounds like. When I'm not around, I will ensure that there is someone around to take care of you, make sure you have nothing to worry about except putting your feet up.'

'You have a house in the country? You've never breathed a word about that. Why?'

Luc chose to ignore question number two. 'House in the country—very relaxing. And here's the thing: a magnificent garden. I think you will find it inspirational.'

He smiled complacently and wondered how long it would take to find a house to fill the spec. Not long, he reckoned. Money could work wonders when it came to things like that.

CHAPTER EIGHT

'I'M STILL not happy with this arrangement.'

Agatha had spent the past eight days at Luc's apartment, having failed to persuade him that she was more than capable of resting in her own place.

'I can't keep an eye on you if you're there,' he had told her with the finality of someone clanging shut an iron door.

Telling him that she had only just moved in, that she was wasting money on rent for a place that was uninhabited, had met with a similarly flat, negative response—although he had made a big show of tilting his head to one side and listening very carefully to every word she was saying.

'You don't need to stress about things like money,' he had assured her with a dismissive wave of his hand. 'Remember what the doctor said.'

His only concession had been to bring her work laptop home for her so that she could fill in some of the long stretches of spare time corresponding with the various customers she had set up in her new role.

Food was prepared for her by a home help which he seemed to have acquired with ridiculous speed, and he had taken to arriving back from work early every evening, although she assured him that there was no need.

Just as he gave one-hundred percent to *everything* he did,

he was giving one-hundred percent to the task of making sure that she didn't lose the baby.

Whilst that felt good, it was also disturbing to know that it was a task to which he had risen because he had had no choice. Had he not found himself thrown into the situation, she would not have laid eyes on him for dust. He had moved on with his life until she had bounced along to turn it on its head.

But what on earth could she do? She didn't want to lose this baby. Her level of attachment to it grew with each passing day. And, secretly, didn't she enjoy being fussed over, never mind that she objected at every turn? Didn't she enjoy lying on the sofa in his living room, watching television with a cup of cocoa in her hand and a stack of magazines at her side and her eyes drifting helplessly from the television to the chair, where Luc sat frowning in concentration at something on his computer? Didn't she enjoy watching him lounge on the two seater next to hers, hands clasped behind his head, making sarcastic comments at some slither of nonsense she had decided to switch on?

Take away the murky undercurrents and the dubious motives, and it was a snapshot of domestic bliss.

At least, as far as *she* was concerned. She had no idea how Luc felt because he was not to be drawn on the subject.

He had been scrupulous in his attentiveness. He had set her up in a guest bedroom and, more than anything else, that seemed to signify his thoughts on her as a responsibility to be heroically borne.

Right now, with her meagre possessions packed and the lease on her small flat cancelled before she had had time to enjoy it, they were speeding along the motorway towards whatever mysterious house in Berkshire he owned.

She had given up asking him too many questions about it and had redirected her efforts towards not succumbing to the tantalising notion that all his efforts at looking after her pointed to a man who was in it for the long haul. It was a seductive but dangerous train of thought, to be avoided at all costs. Loving him made it way too easy for her to be beguiled by mirrors and glass.

'Why not? Why aren't you happy with the arrangement?' Luc didn't glance in her direction. He had had over a week to consider this situation, to realise that the modern-day arrangement she favoured wasn't going to work for him. To work out that, whilst she seemed to appreciate the massive efforts he was making—efforts which were cutting big time into his work life—she had retreated into a shell of sorts, one from which she never ventured to discuss a future. Did she harbour some fear that she would lose the baby? Rest had improved her blood pressure but there was always an outside chance that it might rise again.

'It's like I've been thrown into a tumble drier and tossed around. First you move me into your apartment, even though I told you that I was perfectly okay to look after myself. You decide what I eat. I'm not supposed to lift a finger, and now this—it's like I'm being kidnapped.'

'Needs must. There are women who would appreciate the level of concern.'

Agatha refrained from pointing out that his level of concern had been non-existent the minute she had made the mistake of telling him what she wanted out of their relationship. His level of concern *then* had amounted to a scramble through the nearest exit-door. The wonderful level of concern he was now so eager to demonstrate was to do with the baby she was carrying inside her. She wondered, if and when her pregnancy settled, if he would be quite so assiduous in his attentions.

Which made her think of the future—that great, unmentionable block of time hovering on the horizon. It had become increasingly clear that he was in the process of proving himself good-parent material. He wasn't a fool. He must know that he would need her on his side when it came to the business of visiting rights. Why not start right now to show her just how spectacular he could be in the father stakes when he put his mind to it?

He had clearly decided to carry on with his own life once the baby was born. She had to make a huge effort not to think of him playing happy families with their child while she watched from the sidelines as aspiring bimbos pretended to take a maternal interest. It wouldn't concern him because, in his head, he would have adequately smoothed the way.

'What am I supposed to do in a house in a village where I don't know anyone?'

'You'll know me. I intend to be around a lot.'

'I wish my life was normal again,' Agatha fretted, and he gave her a sharp, sidelong look.

'I find that wishing for the impossible is never a good idea. Life isn't going to be normal for either of us again. We just have to accept that and deal with it.'

'How can you be so...so *practical* about everything?' Agatha almost yelled at him.

'What would you want?'

'I don't know.'

'One of us has to keep a level head and I've nominated myself for the role.' He was driving away from the motorway now. He had been to the house once, but his driver had done the tedious journey while he had worked in the back. Right now, he was keeping an eagle eye on his sat nav and on the road signs, because getting lost might just alert her to the fact that he really didn't know one end of the county from the other; all these little roads down which they were driving had a tendency to look the same.

'What about *my* vote?' Agatha grumbled petulantly, but

she was finding it hard to hold on to her moral high-ground because she was riveted by the scenery. She had forgotten how enticing the countryside was, how clean the air smelled, how technicolour-bright everything seemed to be without the clutter of grey buildings, pavements and smog, and how wonderfully quiet it was, a soft silence unbroken by the sounds of cars and sirens.

'Not counting at the moment,' Luc informed her with that splendid arrogance that she had always found weirdly endearing. 'We're nearly there. Twenty minutes.'

'How often do you come here?' she asked, a question to which he seemed to give an undue amount of consideration before finally saying, 'Not often.'

'And, um, do you usually come here by yourself?' She hadn't wanted to ask the question and she was vaguely surprised that it had somehow found its way out of her mouth.

'Why?'

'No reason. I just find it hard to imagine you being this far out of London on your own and enjoying it.'

'You're the first woman to come here.'

'I wasn't asking if you brought women there.'

'No?' Luc allowed himself a slashing smile, which Agatha saw and which made her want to kick herself. Her state of health had rendered her temporarily helpless and into this uncertain vacuum Luc had muscled his way, taking charge of the reins for the sake of the baby growing inside her. She had to begin the process of stepping away from his control because how else was she going to summon up the necessary strength when she gave birth? Was his plan to keep her emotionally welded to him while he carried on with his life, adopting his role as father without the threat of any other man replacing him because she was still head over heels in love with him?

Luc didn't play by the book. If he had a game plan, then he would see nothing wrong in achieving it by whatever means it took. It was just the way he was built.

He was designed to spot weaknesses and capitalise on them if it suited his ends. It was something she couldn't allow herself to forget.

'It's beautiful here,' she said, changing the uncomfortable subject and looking away from him to stare at the flashing greenery, trees and open fields in which were nestled quaint little towns.

'Isn't it?' Never one to be bowled over by nature, Luc had to agree that there was something restful about the scenery. 'Although rumour has it that places like this are rife with intrigue and scandal.'

Agatha couldn't help herself; she laughed. 'And where did you hear that?'

'I think I gleaned it from all those ridiculous detective shows you insist on watching. Has it escaped you that most of the murders seemed to take place in quiet little backwaters?'

He was irresistible when he used that light, teasing voice. 'I'd better be careful, in that case.'

'No need to worry. I'll be more than careful for the two of us.'

There is no 'two of us'.

They had left all main roads and he glanced across at her as the car swept through some open wooden gates and up a thin, ribbon-like winding drive, bordered on both sides by a profusion of wild flowers that had been artfully planted to emphasise the majesty of the trees around which they nestled.

It was a glorious sight; the estate agent had surpassed himself. Luc had thought that the second he had glimpsed the drive up to the house, and he was reminded of it now.

Money talked, and it had spoken volumes in getting him just the right house to impress.

'Like what you see?' he murmured lazily, driving mega-slowly now so that she could delight in the abundance of flora, a dead cert to have her reeling in pleasant surprise.

When he turned his gaze to her flushed face, he was satisfied that everything was having the desired effect.

She was, quite literally, bowled over.

'Gosh.'

'I know. Stunning, isn't it?'

'I would never have associated you with a place like this in a million years,' Agatha confessed, dragging her eyes away from the marvellous, colourful landscape to briefly focus on him.

'Hidden depths.'

The house was now coming into view, slipping and sliding between the trees. It was not too big and not too small, with whitewashed walls and clambering roses; although there wasn't a picket fence, the low brick wall was covered in ivy and the little gate was wooden. It was a vision of exceptional prettiness that could have leapt from the pages of a story book.

'This is so different from your place in London,' Agatha breathed, her eyes wide like saucers. 'I mean, your place in London is so cold and clinical.'

'A bit like me?' Luc asked, his eyes cooling. He hadn't seen her eyes light up like that since they had been involved all those weeks ago, when she'd been still nursing dreams of permanence.

Agatha shrugged and remembered about all those defences she should be building around her.

'You said it. I didn't.' Then, not wanting to become embroiled in a non-argument, she stared at the approaching house, now in full view, and gasped. 'It's…it's absolutely beautiful, Luc. What a fantastic getaway! I'm surprised you ever want to go back to London after you've been here for a weekend.'

Luc flushed. 'Too much peace can be taxing.'

'Do you have people to look after the garden and stuff?'

'Naturally.'

'Because I can have a go at looking after it for you while I'm here. It would give me something to do.'

'You're here to rest.'

'Gardening *is* restful.'

'I'll take your word on that one,' Luc said drily, drawing to a stop outside the house and moving round to open the passenger door for her. Everything they needed—including all her possessions, and enough equipment for him to work from the house at least part of the time—had been transferred in advance of their arrival. He sensed that he might just go crazy from the solitude, but the town was very close, just beyond the fields at the back, and it was deceptively close to London.

'I suppose it wouldn't do you any harm to potter in the garden. Although no heavy lifting, naturally.'

'Naturally.' She was drinking up the house now with its quirky charm, and thinking how fantastic it was that Luc should even think of owning something like this. He might be as hard as nails when it came to business, and frankly when it came to most things, but just to discover that he had purchased a house like this did indeed point to a sensitive streak in him that made her heart swell.

Inside didn't disappoint. It was beautifully furnished. The sofas were deep and comfortable and all the wood gleamed with the patina of age.

'You must have a brilliant housekeeper,' Agatha remarked, taking in the spotless surfaces and smelling the clean, pine scent of recently polished wood. 'Would you mind if I had a look around?'

Her eyes were sparkling, her cheeks flushed. She was the picture of a woman in love, in this instance with a house. Luc shrugged and nodded, then leaned indolently against the wall, watching as she poked, prodded, disappeared, re-appeared and then ventured up the staircase to where four bedrooms were interspersed higgledy piggledy with two very comfortable bathrooms. Fluffy towels were warming on the towel rails. The beds were all made up with covers of the finest Egyptian cotton. In fact, the house had had a com-prehensive face-lift since he had bought it, so underneath the olde worlde charm it bristled with the shiny sparkle of the brand new.

The cupboards in the kitchen were full to brimming. The freezer was stocked with enough food to keep them going for weeks.

Upstairs, Agatha noted that she had been put in the bed-room furthest away from his and she had to stifle a flash of disappointment. Pinning a bright smile on her face, she wan-dered back downstairs to find him fiddling in the kitchen, and for a few seconds she quietly watched from the doorway. Kitchens perplexed him. He could work every technological gadget on the face of the earth with the exception of those located in a kitchen.

'You really don't need to stay here with me, Luc,' she said from the doorway, and he turned round slowly to look at her with hooded eyes.

In her leggings and oversized shirt, her fair hair tumbling over her shoulders, she looked vulnerable and feminine.

'Tell me something I don't know.'

'You never take time off work. I don't want you feeling that you've got to stay cooped up here because I'm incapable. I'm not. I know this is your house and you must have enjoyed coming here in the past but I bet you never stayed longer than a couple of nights.'

'If I don't look after you, who will? You still haven't told your mother, so she won't be rushing here any time soon.' He knew why she still hadn't said a word to Edith. To break the news would put her in the position of revealing the father's identity. It would also compel her to find reasons to explain why she intended to remain as a single mother. For the moment, he was willing to go along with her silence, but he needed to start manoeuvring things in the direction he wanted them to take.

He abandoned his attempt to work the coffee maker and strolled lazily towards her until he was standing right in front of her.

He moved, she noted absentmindedly, with the sinewy grace of a panther, all dark, dangerous intent. Except she had no idea what he intended. Which didn't stop her heart from pounding like a frenzied drum inside her. Her nipples tightened and she broke out in a fine film of nervous perspiration. How was it that she had never felt so *alone* with him in London, even when she had been bed-bound in his apartment, which was really much smaller? The silence seemed to press against the walls, enclosing them in a little space of their own.

'The time isn't right to tell her,' Agatha mumbled uncertainly, driven to look up at him, even though it was doing dangerous things to her nervous system.

'She's going to wonder where the hell you are when that phone in the flat keeps ringing off the hook and no one answers.'

'I didn't give her the number,' Agatha confessed guiltily, sneaking a glance at him. 'She gets me on my mobile.'

Luc decided to let the matter drop. As he had discovered to his cost, that soft mouth and innocent face belied a stubborn streak that was a match for his own. Nearly.

'I won't be here all of the time, so there's no need to get in a panic. I've employed someone to be here between nine and six, so you'll have company. She'll cook, clean and do whatever else around the house that you want her to. It should give you lots of time to stretch your legs in the garden. Also, she can drive you into town whenever you want, although I won't expect you to go in more than is strictly necessary. In fact, scratch that—if you want to venture into town, I will make myself available to take you there.'

If he was intent on making himself indispensable, then he was going about it the right way, Agatha thought.

'How will you do that?' she asked carefully. 'I thought you said you'd be in London.'

'Some of the time. But it's perfectly possible to conduct business from here. You haven't been to the back of the kitchen, but there's a very passable office space there, and I've kitted it out with everything I need to keep going.'

'You'll go nuts being cooped up here in the middle of nowhere.'

'Then maybe you could distract me,' he dropped into the silence, wondering what she would do with his provocative remark. He hadn't laid a finger on her for weeks. Just at the moment, making love was out of the question, but he could do so many other erotic things with her body...

Could too many cold showers lead to some kind of health risk in a guy? If so, then he was slap bang in the firing line. After his abortive date over a week ago, he had been reluctantly forced to concede that, at least at the moment, he only desired Agatha. It was infuriating but it was undeniable. And even more infuriating was how much he missed her warm, willing body. However much he put his back out to penetrate her friendly but polite façade, he was still uneasily aware that a lot of that façade was there because she just didn't have much of a choice. She wasn't going to bite the hand to which she was temporarily indebted. It was all far from ideal.

Agatha was feverishly wondering what he had meant by it. Was he flirting with her? Trying to ensure that she didn't forget how meaningful he was to her? Laying all her cards on the table had made her vulnerable, and Luc, knowing as much as he did about women, would know precisely the extent of power he wielded over a vulnerable ex-lover. Maybe he thought that the odd word here and there, the occasional look that lingered a little too long, would keep her ensnared so that even without the bonds of marriage there would still be the bonds of emotions left intact.

No way!

'If you want distracting, then my suggestion is that you get out into that beautiful garden,' she said lightly, stepping around any contentious issues and adopting the firm, detached stand she was intent on pursuing. 'I find that always works for me.' She folded her arms and yanked her rebellious imagination back from unsteady images of her distracting him in all sorts of ways that were now one-hundred percent forbidden. 'Especially at this time of year, when it's such lovely weather to really explore what's growing out there. And I noticed an adorable wooden bench under a tree. Maybe you could take your computer out there if you happen to be around. You'll find it very relaxing. And, if it's distraction that you're looking for, then the sounds of the birds in the trees can do the job.'

Eyes narrowing, Luc abruptly turned away. 'Sounds idyllic,' he drawled, recognising the polite dismissal. 'Should I keep a watch out for Snow White and the Seven Dwarves in case they decide to pop into this slice of paradise? I have some work to catch up on. Is there anything you want to know about the house?'

Agatha shook her head, glumly fascinated at how every changing nuance of his moods had such an ability to alter her own. When he was relaxed, she relaxed, even though she knew she should always be on guard. When he was tense, she tensed. When he was attentive, she blossomed inside like a flower opening up to the first rays of the sun. And when like now he withdrew from her, with that cool, shuttered expression on his face, she just wanted to burst into tears and launch into the sort of open-ended, heart-on-sleeve speech that had sent him heading for the hills the first time.

'I'll just have a look around the garden. Then, shall I get something cooked for us to eat later?'

'No need. The freezer has a hundred and one home-cooked meals. I arranged for my chef in London to handle that. And there's ample food in the fridge as well.'

'Do you do that every time you come here?' Agatha asked, driven to hold him in conversation. 'Get your chef to prepare food for you? I guess it saves you having to go out and find somewhere to eat. What's the nearest town like?'

Since Luc had never seen it, he had to think quickly on his feet, coming up with something so stupendously vague that she was left more in the dark after his reply than she had been before it: post office. A few shops—and why would he know what ones, because he had no interest in exploring them. A pub or two. The usual. Weren't all these small, rural towns and villages much the same? he decided on the spot.

'So if you don't go into the town very often, and you really aren't into gardens, what was the appeal?'

'This is beginning to sound like the Spanish Inquisition.'

'I'm sorry. I don't mean it to. I was just curious. I mean...' She continued awkwardly as she tried to backpedal rapidly away from giving the impression that she was over-interested—or else, worse, clinging to conversation because when he wasn't around something inside her went out, like a light switch being dimmed. 'If we're going to be cooped up here together off and on, then it would be nice for us to keep the conversation light.'

Several things in that one sentence annoyed the hell out of Luc: 'cooped up', 'off and on', and 'light conversation', to be precise.

'As you may have noticed,' Luc said through gritted teeth, 'It's peaceful here. It makes a change.' He had purchased this quaint little house with a plan in sight. Now his subterfuge was beginning to cause him some disquiet. He hadn't banked on being quizzed over something as innocuous as owning a place in the country. He owned several apartments—one in New York, another in Paris and three in London which he used, occasionally, for visiting clients. What was the big deal?

'I think it's really great that you get away from work sometimes,' Agatha confided. 'Working too hard is bad for a person.'

'I think we part company on that one, Agatha.' Luc remembered just why he had been forced to break off their relationship in the first place. He reminded himself of the folly of a man like him—driven and entirely focused on his work and on the rigorous demands of having to run a multi-billion-pound empire—ever contemplating a relationship with any woman who saw the need to rein him back. Applying his intellect brought him back down to earth: he was here for a reason. She was carrying his baby, and when that baby was born he fully intended to be the sole father figure in its life. No sideline job. No visiting rights. And a ring on her finger so that there would be no temptation for her to imagine that there was a single life out there beckoning.

'Right. Yes. We do.' His coolly delivered words had the same effect as a bucket of cold water being thrown over her, and Agatha blushed and turned away. 'I'll go explore the garden,' she said in a stilted voice. Then, before he could remind her that she was a fragile piece of spun glass that needed careful handling because *his baby* depended on it, she added, irritably, 'And there's no need for you to worry. You won't have to rescue me because I've over-exerted myself by having a five-second stroll!'

But it was hardly the peaceful stroll she would have wanted. Everything around her was sumptuous, but her head was a whirlwind of tangled thoughts, and the more she picked away at them, the more tangled they became.

After half an hour, and with the temperature beginning to drop, she returned to the house, only glancing across at the kitchen on her way to the stairs. Once Luc was ensconced in front of his computer, wild horses wouldn't be able to drag him away, and she needed some time to herself.

In the corner of the room, her emptied suitcase had been tucked away under a pretty trestle table which housed an ornate, flowered jug in its matching bowl. Wandering into the adjoining bathroom, she saw the immaculate towels and an array of bath products that would have been worthy of the most expensive hotel in the world. All brand new. But, then again, why shouldn't they be? Luc hadn't said how often he visited this place, but she suspected not very, and he wouldn't want to find himself using products that had been hardened over time from lack of use.

She began running the bath, and it was only when it was run and the air was fragrant with the rose-petal smell from the bubble bath that she noticed the glaring absence of any lock on the door.

And on the bedroom door.

Old house, she thought, dismayed. Fantastically modern in all aspects except for this one.

But her room was far from his. He was currently lost in some intricacy to do with business. And she wasn't going to be long.

The weight of the anxiety she had tried to bury seeped out of her as she settled her now slightly more ungainly body into the bath, relaxing with a sigh into the foam and closing her eyes.

On the plus side it was undeniably good to be out of London, even taking into account the efforts she had made to relocate herself to somewhere a little less cramped. It was, however, the only plus that sprang to mind. Hot on its heels were a series of towering minuses; starting with the fact that she was now hopelessly dependent on a man who had only weeks previously turned his back on her, and ending with the miserable suspicion that there was more to his grand displays of attentiveness than he was letting on.

She had the trapped feeling of something very small and vulnerable slowly being circled by a much bigger, much cleverer predator.

And how was she going to deal with it? She could be entirely wrong about everything, and Luc might, just might, have turned into Mr Nice Guy, but even in her wildest dreams she found that difficult to get her head around.

Had she dozed off just for a few seconds? Had she been having a dream that involved her clutching a posy of flowers, just like the ones in the rambling garden outside, watching as Luc smiled down at some other woman in front of an altar before slipping a ring on her finger?

The clarity of the dream jerked her awake. Or was it the sound of the door being pushed open?

In the first few confused seconds of disorientation, the figure of Luc by the bathroom door was like the manifestation of her dream. Except this manifestation wasn't smiling. His mouth was drawn into a tight, grim line and his eyes glittered in the subdued lighting in the bathroom.

Agatha gave a little squeak of horror when the manifestation spoke, and she struggled into a sitting position, dazed, flushed and staring wide-eyed like a rabbit suddenly caught in the headlights of a speeding car.

'Where the hell have you been?'

Agatha's mouth fell open and she heard herself stammer something about a stroll and the garden and then a bath. In spreading dismay, she realised that the bath water was now tepid and the bubbles had disappeared, leaving her exposed to Luc's raking green eyes.

With his blood pressure back to normal now that he had managed to locate her, Luc took in the scene that confronted him. And what a glorious picture it was. A now slightly more rounded Agatha was frantically trying to hide herself, but there was only so much two hands could do, and his eyes feasted on the smooth swell of her belly, the fullness of her breasts. He had dreamt of this and his body reacted as though a thousand volts of electricity had suddenly been shot through it. He almost lost his cool completely and groaned out loud. Instead, he moved swiftly towards her.

'You're shivering!' He dipped his hand into the water and grimaced. 'It's stone cold!'

'I must have nodded off.' Agatha stared at him helplessly. In the faded jeans in which he had traveled, and an equally faded rugby jumper harking back to his university days, Luc was drop-dead gorgeous. She would have given anything for him not to have had this effect on her but there was no denying the stirring she felt between her thighs and the way her nipples tightened and hardened, standing to immediate, aroused attention.

'Do you call this taking care of yourself?' Luc growled.

With no escape-route handy, she felt herself scooped out of the water and deposited gently on the ground. And because something appeared to have happened to her legs, making it impossible for them to move, she was a very naked and willing recipient of one of the large, fluffy towels that had been hanging on the heated towel-rail.

'I've been out in that bloody garden for the last thirty minutes hunting you down!' he delivered with biting reproach, as he once again swept her off her feet, kicking open the bathroom door and heading towards the king-sized bed. 'I've been worried sick!'

CHAPTER NINE

'YOU'VE been *worried*?' Agatha couldn't stop the tingle of delight that gathered in the pit of her stomach at those telling words. In fact, the feeling obscured the very fact that she was still naked, wrapped in the towel and sharing the same space as Luc: three things that should have had her running for cover.

'You should have informed me the minute you got back inside the house.'

'You were working. I didn't want to disturb you. Besides, I didn't think that I was supposed to clock in and clock out like one of the temps in your office!' Noticeably, he had dropped the 'worried sick' line of chat. Maybe he thought that an admission like that, an admission that might just possibly border on the not-entirely unemotional, would give her inappropriate ideas: ideas that he cared about her, when he patently didn't.

'It occurred to me that you might have got lost in the garden. It looks small, but there's acres of it, and quite a bit of it is woodland. With the sun going down, it would be difficult for you to find your way around.' That cool explanation was a far cry from the sudden pounding panic he had felt when he had walked round and round, calling her name with ever more urgency, imagining her merrily getting lost in the sprawling countryside like Gretel, but without the trail of breadcrumbs to find her way back home.

Rage, that she should take such little effort to look after herself, when she had been warned often and well about the necessity of doing so, was easier to deal with.

He had been flipping his phone open, ready to call the local police, when he had decided to do a check of the house.

Pushing open the bathroom door had been the last resort, for he had again called her name various times and received no response.

Little wonder when she had fallen asleep in the bath! How long had she been there? 'Are you beginning to warm up?' he asked gruffly and she nodded and pulled the towel tightly around her.

'You need to change,' he said, moving towards her. 'You'll catch some kind of chill otherwise.'

Agatha was tempted to tell him not to be foolish, but what leg did she have to stand on when she had slept in a cold bath for heaven only knew how long? Now, instead of getting her act together and putting on her adult hat, she was yawning, feeling sleepy again and not really wanting to do anything except look at him and savour the concern etched into his harsh, beautiful features.

'This is *exactly* why you can't be left on your own,' he fulminated grimly, searching through her drawers and coming up with underwear, a tee-shirt and a pair of stretchy jogging bottoms. He turned to look at her darkly. 'What if you'd been on your own and fallen asleep in the bath?'

'I expect I would have woken up eventually, a little wrinkled and a little cold.'

'The doctor said you're to take it easy. Freezing half to death in a bath because you've nodded off isn't taking it easy by anyone's standards.'

Agatha was only half-taking in what he was saying. She was fixated by the way he was moving towards the bed, her clothes in his hands and an expression of intent on his face.

'Wh...what are you doing?' she squeaked, when the mattress depressed under his weight as he sat next to her on the bed.

In truth, Luc wasn't entirely sure. He was only now coming down from his extraordinary flight of panic. He looked down at her upturned face and frowned.

He was taking charge, he thought, as the fog cleared. It was what he did. And good thing too, because she certainly seemed to be pretty poor at it. He swept aside the memory of that sickening rush that had overwhelmed him when he had gone outside to look for her. Instead, he focused on the potential hazard she posed to herself and their unborn baby.

He hooked his finger under the towel where she had pulled it tight across her breasts and felt the whoosh of her sharply indrawn breath. But, although she reached to cover his hand with hers, her eyes remained locked with his; what he read there gave the lie to her pitiful show of brushing him off.

'I...I can dress myself, Luc.' Agatha heard the breathlessness in her voice with a sense of dismay. The warmth of his finger nestling in her cleavage was scorching hot against her skin. When she shivered compulsively, she prayed that he might mistakenly jump to the conclusion that she was still cold after her silly experience in the bath.

The hot flare in his eyes told her that, whatever conclusion he had jumped to, it certainly wasn't the wrong one and she felt an answering leap in her pulses that didn't surprise her. Why should it? Even when she had been giving herself long lectures about staying away from him because he was bad for her health—even when she had told herself that he was only out to manipulate her because it suited him to have her firmly anchored under his thumb—she had still been susceptible to that ferocious charm of his and frighteningly undone by a love she hadn't been able to sweep under the carpet.

How hard had she fought to hang on to her independence once she had discovered that she was pregnant? She might not have succumbed to his marriage proposal, because not all of her pride had been squashed into the ground, but the second her health had given cause for concern she had allowed him to step into the breach and take over.

And Luc could offer degree courses on taking over. Before she had had time to think straight, she had been moved lock, stock and barrel into his apartment and then, in the space of a heartbeat, here to his country house.

Her protests had been so ineffectual that it was little wonder that they had been comprehensively ignored.

A shameful sense of guilt assailed her because she *liked* having his finger touching her like a branding iron.

It took little more than a gentle tug to free her hand from its limp hold and for the towel to fall to the bed.

Agatha stared at the discarded puddle of towelling with an air of disassociation.

'You're carrying my baby.' Luc's velvety voice was a notch lower. 'I want to see how it's shaping your body.'

The sound of his voice snapped her back to reality and she made an attempt to scrabble for the towel, but he closed his hand around one slender wrist, pinning her in mid-movement.

'Please, Agatha.'

'This is inappropriate,' she breathed unevenly.

'Is it? I've seen you naked before.'

'But we don't have that kind of relationship now!'

'Your breasts are bigger.' He was vaguely surprised that he could speak at all, because the sight of her was breath-taking. Literally, he felt as though the breath had been driven out of his body.

He reached out and cupped her breast, feeling the naked weight of it in his hands, and it was as though her body had been trained to react in a certain inevitable way to his touch. She fell back against the pillows, her eyelids fluttering as a wave of heat stole through her body, sending her entire system in full crash mode.

'And your nipples are bigger as well. And darker. Is that normal?'

'Luc...'

'I like it when you say my name like that,' he confessed in a ragged, unsteady voice.

There was no way that making love fully was an option but he still wanted her with every fibre of his being.

'This is so not right...'

'How can it be *not* right?' he murmured, briefly glancing at her face, but driven to look again at her even more bountiful body. 'You're pregnant with my baby. How can it not be right for me to look at you? But of course, if you want me to go, then I will...' It was a chance, but he was a gambler, and he always knew his game. The gentle quiver of her body under his raking inspection told him all that he needed to know and the curling of her fingers now in his springy hair was confirming it.

Instead of triumph, however, he just felt a bone-deep sense of peace as he traced the outline of her nipple with a wandering finger and then moved on to circle her smooth, rounded stomach. She could still get away with wearing jeans, but to his sharp eyes she had changed in a thousand little ways, from the shape and size of her breasts and nipples to the infinitesimal thickening of her waistline. Already she was beginning to put on a little weight and it suited her. It was incredibly sexy to think that all of this was due to his own flesh and blood inside her. Having never really given the question of issue a passing thought, he now wondered what the sex of the baby would be. Boy or girl? Dark hair, he imagined. Wasn't that a genetic trait that superceded the fair-haired gene?

The need to weld her to him was intense. In a little over six months she would give birth to his child, a son or a daughter; it bordered on obscene to think of another man entering her life.

That thought gave an edge to his roaming hands. When he bent to lick her big, dark nipples and he felt her squirm under him, he felt a rush of satisfaction and purpose.

'No making love,' he said ruefully, standing to remove his clothing and keeping his eyes pinned on her avid, flushed face. 'But I can still touch. Would you like that? Would you find it de-stressing?' He stepped out of his jeans, kicking them to one side, and pulled off the rugby shirt in one swift, fluid movement.

Agatha felt like someone deprived of food and sustenance for way too long suddenly confronted with a banquet. Her senses seemed to reach overload with shocking ease as she drank in the long, lean lines of his body. Assurance was in his every move as he ditched the boxer shorts and stood completely naked in front of her, proud, beautiful and clearly turned on.

She shifted when he slipped into bed with her, pushing aside the covers and looking at her with such open hunger that she wriggled under the scrutiny.

'This isn't supposed to happen,' she whispered, reaching out for sanity one last time before it disappeared altogether—then immediately contradicting her valiant words when she traced the exquisite line of his sensuous mouth with a wayward, rebellious finger.

Luc didn't answer. He gave her a slow, curling smile and then captured her finger, only to circle it with his mouth and suck gently on it while he locked his eyes on her surprised face.

He shifted a little so that she could feel what she was doing to him, heavy and urgent against her leg.

Still very gently, he moved to give the rest of her body the attention it deserved.

Agatha, caught up in a maelstrom of strong feelings and powerful sensation, could no more have fought his seductive onslaught than she could have hitched a ride to the moon. Her body responded to the lazy flick of his tongue on her nipple by heating up, yet seemingly turning to jelly. Her legs relaxed and fell open and she closed her eyes on a sigh of intense pleasure as his tongue teased and licked a burning path from one engorged nipple to the next.

Still exploring her sensitised breasts, he cupped one hand between her thighs and then slowly rubbed her, feeling her moisture like honeyed dew on his fingers until she came apart under his touch.

There was no need for him to guide her hand to him. Half-curling on her side to face him, she took him and played with him so that his hardness became as solid as steel, and he groaned and shuddered.

'I think,' he delivered unevenly, 'That I am just about to have the safest sex known to mankind.'

Far more satisfying it would have been to be able to plunge into the wet depths of her and feel her silky dampness around his sheath, but all in good time... For now, he released himself to the rhythm of her sure hand and then sank back against the pillow for a matter of a few seconds, spent, just catching his breath before giving her a wry look.

'What does it say that that was better than anything with any other woman?'

Leaving her little time to ponder that revealing reflection, he drew her gently against him.

'You can completely relax here,' he murmured soothingly into her ear. 'No need to stack up your defences. As you see, we don't have to be at war with one another. I'm a peaceful kind of guy.' He stroked her thigh and Agatha was content to gaze into those fabulous eyes and go along for the ride. 'Life,' he continued with satisfaction in his voice, 'will be infinitely more enjoyable if we can bury our differences and accept one another.'

'You mean climb into bed together?' She was beginning to review exactly what she had done and she didn't like the slow-motion picture show that was taking place in her head. But waging war with that was the seductive pull of her senses, telling her that letting him into her life like this wasn't necessarily a bad thing—was it? She had to think and she slowly eased herself away from him.

'Where are you going?'

'I need to have something to eat. I'm really hungry.'

'Now? Right this instant?'

Feet already firmly planted on the ground, Agatha nodded without looking at him. 'I'm wide awake now.'

'Wait. You don't know the layout of the place.'

'It's not that big, Luc. I think I can find my way to the kitchen and locate the fridge. If food's already been cooked, it won't test my intelligence too much to stick it on the stove.'

Luc, who had been keenly enjoying the drowsy warmth of her surrender, frowned at the subtle change of mood. Then he decided that mood swings were all part and parcel of the pregnancy process, and the fact that she had finally acknowledged what they both knew to be a fact was all that mattered. The house, which had seemed the last word in self-imposed exile—so distant from all the things he took for granted, namely the buzz of civilization—now seemed a lot more palatable. He hadn't realised how much he had missed touching her and feeling her curled against him. He also hadn't realised how much he had missed having her around him, warm, content and compliant.

'I'll join you in a while. I'm going to have a shower and I need to make a couple of calls to the office. And don't worry...' He grinned and held up his hands in mock surrender, as though she had protested. 'I'll make them here and I'll be all yours when I join you in the kitchen.'

Agatha smiled weakly back at him and climbed back into her clothes. Her body was still tingling in all the places he had touched and it maddened her that he had that effect on her. She wondered whether she had known all along that sooner or later she would end up back in bed with him. She wondered whether that tantalising prospect had formed the basis of her acquiescence to all his manipulations.

Mostly she was utterly confused at the thought of what happened next.

How could she pull back now and start preaching about being just friends? How could she get sniffy and talk about being adults, pretending that what had happened had just been a little oversight?

In a state of utter turmoil, she left him in the bedroom and wandered downstairs to the kitchen, switching on lights as she went and distracted from her train of thoughts by her real appreciation of the house. It was a house designed for someone who enjoyed exploring, because the rooms were small, quirky and quaint and all invited inspection. Rich, expensive rugs interrupted the polished parquet-flooring and there were a number of open fires in various rooms. In the depths of winter, she could imagine curling up with a book on one of the big, comfy chairs with a log fire burning, the world safely locked out.

But she realised that none of that was going to happen. She was a temporary visitor to this idyll. She didn't even know how long she would be here. A date for departure hadn't been mentioned but she was stronger now and fast approaching a time when she would be able to return to London and, to work part-time at least, if not full-time. She wouldn't need Luc around keeping his beady eye on her to make sure that she didn't do another falling-asleep-in-the-bath routine. Should she just go with the flow while she was here? Give in to the disastrous craving to be touched by him and then establish the necessary distance when she was back in London and away from his stifling presence?

She feverishly wondered whether she should have accepted his offer of a marriage of convenience when he had first made it instead of deluding herself into thinking that she was worth more than that. If she couldn't get a grip on her responses to him, if she was destined to lead a life in thrall to a man who didn't love her, then shouldn't she just have stuck the ring on her finger and legalised her foolishness?

And then there was the problem of her mother, whom she had yet to tell about the pregnancy. What was she going to say about her daughter going it alone when she had been given the option of financial stability and security from a guy who was—in her mother's eyes—perfect husband-material?

The whole chaotic mess swirled round and round in her head as she browsed through the fridge for food, finally deciding on chicken salad and some bread.

And then, more because there was no sound of Luc coming downstairs rather than nosiness, she walked through the kitchen and into the room behind it which he had told her he used as his office.

It was a honeycomb rather than a traditional office-space; yet again she was struck that he could be as at home in surroundings like that as in his own super-modern offices in London.

Everything needed for work was housed in the biggest of the spaces, a square room that overlooked the garden through a massive bay-window. Dominating the room was his desk, which was old, large and so highly polished that she could practically see her reflection on its surface when she gazed down.

A quick glance told her that there was also a sitting room, comfortably furnished with a little sofa and a couple of chairs. It was saved from having the look of a waiting room by the opulence of the Persian rug in the middle and a low sideboard that looked astronomically expensive. A bathroom completed the series of rooms. Impressed with what she saw, she was about to leave to check the food when Luc's open briefcase caught her eye; on the very top, screaming at her, was what resembled a brochure.

Agatha was not nosy by nature; she didn't pry into things that didn't concern her. But, the very second she spotted that brochure, she knew that she had to look at it because, really, what would Luc be doing with brochures? If he wanted a holiday, he had people who sorted it out for him. He only had to snap his fingers. In fact, if he wanted a cup of coffee he had only to snap his fingers. So why would he bother doing something as mundane as sourcing a travel brochure to anywhere?

Was he, maybe, going to surprise her with a trip somewhere? She squashed that treacherous thought before it could take root and guiltily took the brochure from the case.

It took a few seconds, then the dull pain of recognition washed through her.

There, on page two of the brochure, in all its glory, was

the house in which she was now standing. The estate agent was effusive about all the wonderful things that charming corner of Berkshire had to offer—and was even more effusive in its praise for the only-just-refurbished period house recently on the market which was, it would seem, a jewel. She stared down at the little snapshots of the various rooms which she had been admiring only minutes earlier.

She had had difficulty imagining Luc ever being at home in a house like this. He was a man born to live in the fast lane; a charming little place in the middle of nowhere would have been anathema to him.

Yet, even knowing this, she had still chosen to side-step the obvious and give him the benefit of the doubt, convince herself that his choice of second home showed a side of him that was calmer, more laid back and less aggressively fuelled for the cut and thrust of running an empire.

She must have been self-delusional! The house had been bought for a purpose and the purpose had been just what she had feared all along: Luc didn't want *her*, he wanted his baby, and the fastest way to ensure total control without the messiness of a marriage he had rapidly decided against was to make sure that she remained in his power. Like a complete fool, she had danced to his tune and how hard had he had to try? He knew which buttons to press when it came to her, and he had ruthlessly used that knowledge to break down her defences. Dream house, dream garden...*bingo*.

She hesitated and then, with the throb of an impending headache behind her eyes, she clasped the house details and quietly headed back up to her bedroom, turning off the stove on the way.

It was a relief to find her bedroom empty. Luc had either disappeared back to his own room to change or else to make his precious phone calls.

Having dithered about what she was going to do, how

she was going to break free of the power he had over her, Agatha was now calmly aware of what she needed to do.

She needed to leave; finding that brochure had clarified everything in her head. Luc didn't love her and he never had. Being tempted into bed with him wasn't just a sign of weakness, it was a suicide mission as far as her heart went, not to mention her chances of moving ahead with her life.

Having had him walk in on her in the middle of a bath, she was reluctant to have another, so instead she pulled her suitcase out and began stuffing her clothes inside.

She was in the middle of clearing out her meagre supply of cosmetics and cramming them into a little flowered bag when the bedroom door was pushed open and she stilled, her hand hovering above the bag, before she shoved the mascara in and slowly turned to face him.

His hair was still damp from his shower and he had changed into some black jeans and a black tee-shirt which, combined, gave him the look of a pirate. He exuded sexiness, lounging against the door frame with his arms folded and his deep-green eyes shuttered.

All over again, Agatha felt that burning, frightening response that rebelled against all her efforts to put it away. Prickles of awareness shot through her body and she stuck her hands behind her back and twined her fingers nervously together.

'What's going on?' It emerged as less of a question than a demand for information in the face of what was utterly incomprehensible.

For some reason, she had frozen him out, but Luc had convinced himself that it was a passing mood swing; he had returned to the bedroom, having first checked the kitchen, with his fine spirits fully restored. He had made his calls and had decided to put work on the back burner for the remainder of the day. He might, he had thought with a mixture of surprise and amusement, even consider taking a little break altogether. After all, the house had not come cheap, so why not take some time out to explore all the nooks and crannies of the town with which he was supposed to have at least a passing acquaintance? All in all, it was an enjoyable prospect.

'I'm leaving.'

Shock lanced through him but he was determined to keep that overblown response to himself.

'No,' he said calmly. 'You're not.'

'Don't you dare tell me what I can and can't do! I'm sick of it. I'm sick of you thinking that you can do whatever you please because you think that you're always right!'

'I know what's best for you, and getting all worked up isn't.'

On that score, Agatha grudgingly conceded to herself that he was right. She breathed in deeply and tried to gather her scattered emotions. 'No, Luc, you don't know what's best for *me*, you know what's best for *you* and you'll do anything within your power to make sure that you get what's best for you. That's just the way you've conditioned yourself to approach life. You treat human beings like pieces on a chess board that you can move around, like life is just one big game and you get to control how it's played.'

Luc flushed darkly. Instinctively, he reared up against the criticism. Not for the first time, he marvelled at the temerity of any woman who had no qualms about stampeding all over the boundaries he had in place around him. Agatha didn't care a jot about tiptoeing around his sensibilities. She spoke what was on her mind with the forceful directness of a laser-guided missile homing in on whatever target had been set.

His response to that full-on attack should have been immediate, cold withdrawal but that was an option he barely stopped to consider.

He was discomforted by the accuracy of her criticism but he wasn't going to dwell on that. Right now, his main objective was to get her to calm down, and with that in mind he took a few cautious steps towards her, treading as warily as someone on a mission to disarm a live bomb.

With the memory of that hateful brochure burning brightly in her head, Agatha stood her ground and placed her hands on her hips, leaning forward with glaring hostility.

'You need to calm down,' he said soothingly, stopping just short of putting his hands on her arms because there was a very real suspicion that any physical contact might just have the opposite effect and send her into complete meltdown.

'There's something I want to show you.' She turned away abruptly and made for her handbag into which she had stuck the brochure where it could be a constant reminder of his deception—just in case there ever came a time when she found her resolve weakening.

Luc knew exactly what he was looking at the second she held out her hand and he paled.

Watching him through narrowed eyes, Agatha detected that fleeting sign of guilt, and it felt like the death knell to all the hopes she had cherished in varying degrees over the time she had known him.

'Where did you get that?'

'It was lying at the top of your briefcase.'

'You shouldn't have been snooping around.'

'I wasn't snooping around. Your briefcase was wide open. Not that it matters anyway. Why did you lie to me? Why did you tell me that this was a second house? Do you know, I actually believed you. How dumb was I?'

She had promised herself that she would act cool and collected, that she would tell him about the house if he pressed her for a reason for her sudden, pressing need to leave. Which, of course, he would: as she had been foolish enough to hop back into bed with him, he would have been riding high on the optimistic assumption that she was once more his for the asking. When she thought about that, she just wanted to dig a hole, jump in and lie low for a thousand years.

'Okay. So I led you to believe that this was one of my other homes.'

'You didn't *lead me to believe.* You openly lied to me!'

'Does it matter?' He gave a careless shrug while Agatha watched him with jaw-dropping incredulity. He had just admitted lying to her and he still had the nerve to stand there, cool as a cucumber, and act as though it didn't matter.

'It matters to *me*!' Agatha managed to impart through tightly gritted lips.

'Why? You were in a fragile state and you needed somewhere to de-stress. I provided that place. Frankly, from my point of view, you should be thanking me.' Yes, he had been momentarily disconcerted by her attack, but now he was regrouping fast, keeping it all very controlled, speaking in a low, placating voice, trying to find the right words from a vocabulary that seemed strangely limited.

'*I* should be thanking *you*?' Agatha gazed at him in utter, helpless bewilderment.

'London was no place for you to be, not when you needed to rest. You would have been tempted to work, go out, alleviate the boredom of being cooped up. My apartment is comfortable enough, but there's no outside area. You needed a house. Somewhere peaceful. I took that on board and supplied it. What was wrong with that? What was wrong with putting your needs first?'

Agatha thought bitterly that all he needed at this point was the sound of angels and the playing of a harp. At face value, everything he said seemed to demonstrate the actions of a pious, caring guy—but what about all the things that were being left unsaid?

'You knew I didn't want to be in debt to you, Luc. You knew,' she added in a barely audible mumble, 'that I wanted to get over you...'

With that declaration out in the open, Luc at last felt that he had something to get his teeth into. 'But you haven't, have you?' he asked bluntly. 'What we did upstairs proves that, Agatha, and what's the point in running away from the obvious?'

'Did you bring me here with that at the back of your mind, Luc? Did you arrange this whole cottage thing because you knew how I felt about you? Was this perfect dream-house a cynical tool in your plans to seduce me?' Shamefully, she realised how close she had been to falling back in love with a perfect outcome. He had appealed to her most basic desires by producing a house he had known she would adore. The cruelty of the ruse was a bitter pill to swallow.

There were a thousand ways of answering that question and the most sensible choice, given her present state of mind, would have been a rapid and assured denial—but such a denial seemed suddenly impossible to voice.

'It crossed my mind that we might just end up back in bed together.'

Agatha balled her hands into fists and shot him a look of pure loathing, before staring down at her feet and counting to ten to clear some of the red mist in her head.

'I'm being honest here. I...Okay, I really missed you when you were gone. I still want you and I'm not ashamed of that.'

Agatha had an insane urge to burst out into hysterical laughter. He *missed* her! Missed her *so much*, she thought, that he had compensated by making sure not to beat a path to her door—in fact to start seeing another woman! He was all too happy to talk about still wanting her—wanting her enough, in fact, to go out and buy a house for a ridiculous sum of money. Anything to ensure that she was well and truly emotionally shackled to him, so that when she was he would then be free to release his stranglehold and pick up where he had left off with other women, knowing that she would find it impossible to replace him.

'Well, I *am* ashamed,' she said, with weariness creeping into her voice. 'And I'm mortified that I did end back up in bed with you, because you're no good for me. You're attractive, Luc, no one's going to deny that—and I'm only human, after all. But I don't feel proud of myself sleeping with you. I feel like I've let myself down.'

'Don't say that!' A sickening sense of the unreal swept over him like a tidal wave. Plans and expectations were being unpicked by the second but Luc really had no idea how to put a stop to the rapid unravelling.

'Okay. I won't. But I want to leave. Will you drive me to the station? Course, you have no idea where it is.' She gave him a tight, bitter smile. 'You may have to use your sat nav.'

CHAPTER TEN

SHE planned on going home, back to see her mother, the bearer of unexpected tidings. Of course, Luc was not going to allow her to catch a train.

'You've taken leave of your senses if you think I'm going to let you make that journey on your own on public transport,' he said determinedly, watching with a peculiar sensation of falling as she carried on flinging the remainder of her possessions into the case sprawled on the bed.

'You can't *make* me do anything, Luc.'

'I wouldn't put that to the test, if I were you.'

'Or else what?'

'I'm not above keeping you here until you calm down.'

'You wouldn't dare!'

'Don't you know that you should never say something like that to a man like me?' He shook his head and uttered a strangled, frustrated sound under his breath. 'Why don't you have a bath and then we'll talk?'

'Talk about what? Talk about the way you engineered this whole situation?' She could feel herself getting heated up all over again and she did the deep-breathing exercise thing and tried not to focus on the humiliation of having been taken for a ride, an easy conquest for a man who was out to stamp his authority over her bid for freedom.

She was also trying not to feel disappointed at the thought

of leaving the house. It was fabulous, and just exactly the sort of place she adored, even if it had been bought as a means to an end.

'I should have known that you would be the last person on the face of the earth to ever have a house like this!' she blurted out, her eyes stinging. With a sense of tired defeat, she sat on the small stool by the dressing table and watched guardedly as he took up position on the bed, pushing the open suitcase out of the way.

'Meaning?' Luc wondered whether she had any idea just how damned unpredictable she was, like a thoroughbred race-horse prone to spooking at the slightest opportunity. He was watching her very carefully now, his expression unreadable but missing nothing as the bright, feverish flush in her cheeks began to fade slightly.

He had to keep her engaged in talking to him, without the contentious issue of the house acting as a wedge and ramping up her emotions. Retrospectively he wondered whether he should have told her about the house, perhaps allowed her in on the decision-making process, shown her proof positive that he wasn't going to do a runner. Should he have done that? Unused to questioning himself, he attempted to bolster his decision to do what he had done by reminding himself that he had acted in good faith—and, really, what was wrong in employing all the means at his disposal to facilitate that event? Since when was it a crime to lever the odds in your favour?

'Since when are you the type to like small rooms, old-fashioned furniture and outdoor space? I must have been a fool to have ever bought in to your story about coming here for weekends. You don't *like* getting away from your twenty-four-hours-a-day work days! Why would you need rest and relaxation in a cottage out in the country? You don't know *how* to rest and relax! And, if you *did* want to get away for a few seconds, why would you choose to come to a place like this when you could spend a fortune and go to a hotel somewhere with Internet access and all mod cons?'

Luc gave the question some thought and then raised his eyebrows with a wry, mocking smile. 'Funnily enough, it doesn't seem as claustrophobic as I'd imagined.'

'I just don't understand how you could deceive me.'

'I'm going to run a bath for you.'

'That's not an answer!'

'I know. Come on.'

'I'm not going to have a bath with you around,' Agatha said, blushing furiously when she remembered just what had got her sitting here, mortified and angry with herself for having climbed back into bed with him again.

'I wouldn't expect you to.' Although he was pretty sure that, if she did emerge with nothing but a towel around her, neither of them would be able to help themselves. He left her sitting by the dressing table, giving her time to cool down and making sure that the bath was as fragrant and as tempting as possible. He emerged from the adjoining bathroom five minutes later to find her still on the stool, which was highly satisfactory, as a plausible alternative would have seen her trying to lug her case off the bed and transport it to the door. There was very little he would put past her.

'What are you going to do with the house when I've gone?' was the first thing she threw at him.

'Talking to you is beginning to resemble walking on broken glass,' Luc said, holding in his patience with a tight rein whilst simultaneously wondering how it was that this woman could sabotage his ability for self-control without even trying. He raked his fingers through his hair and shook his head as though trying to clear his thoughts. 'Whatever I say, you're going to interpret in the worst possible light. I've done my utmost to take care of your needs. I bought this house because I knew it was the sort of thing you liked. I could imagine you relaxing in the garden a hundred miles away from all the stress and chaos in London. And you do like the house and you do like the garden—so how is it that I've suddenly become the villain of the piece? So we made love. You wanted it as much as I did.' Frustration threatened to boil over.

'That was before I worked out that everything you did was designed to get me into bed! It's like you blackmailed me. It's like…like you took my dreams and manipulated them to get what you wanted.'

'Agatha, go and have your bath.' *Was that the best he could do?* Where was that legendary talent for persuasion when he needed it most? He turned away; she could have thrown something at that dark, lean, handsome head of his. Instead she gave an inarticulate sound of pure resentment and stood up, shaking like a leaf.

'And when I come out I want to be dropped to the station!'

'I'll do better than that. I'll drive you to your mother's house.'

'Good!' She had made her point and got her own way. So why was she feeling miserable? 'And I don't want you hanging around in here while I have a bath!'

'Fine.'

'And don't even *think* of bursting in on me! There's no lock on the wretched door.'

'The down side of some old houses. I won't burst in on you unless I suspect that you've decided to have a snooze. And just for the record, whether you like it or not, or believe me or not, I care about your welfare.'

He *cared about her welfare.* Agatha swallowed back the pressing temptation to ask how he could be so unemotional while she felt like a volcano on the verge of eruption. But why would she ever suspect that he could be otherwise? His capacity for passion was channelled into work and into sex and he had never pretended that between those two opposing poles there was anything else. He had never said a word to her, ever, about love, affection, need—not even in the heat of the moment when all barriers were down and endearments uttered only to be later sheepishly retrieved. Even when their bodies were entwined, and they were scaling heights that had left her breathless and weak, his inherent self-control was always in place.

How could she still love a man like that? How could she build up all her defences and then allow them to drop the second he laid a finger on her? Where was her pride and sense of self-worth?

Luc, keeping it calm, was angrily aware that somewhere inside there was a seething, whirling pool of turmoil that was threatening every principle by which he ruled his life. He was also aware that he didn't like it when she retreated the way she was retreating now. He liked her clingy and needy. It was a disturbing notion, and he didn't know what to do with it, so instead he chose to focus on the practicalities. He would drive her to her mother's house. It would be a long, arduous and boring trip but it would give him time to come up with a plan B now that plan A had failed so spectacularly. He had no doubt that there would be a plan B because he was nothing if not clever when it came to getting exactly what he wanted.

'If you don't mind leaving…' Agatha said haughtily and Luc shot her a frown from under his lashes, hovering for a few seconds before turning on his heels and striding out of the door. But even downstairs, sitting in the kitchen with his laptop in front of him, he couldn't concentrate on his reports, updates and emails.

He gave her exactly half an hour and then he headed up

the stairs, making sure to make sufficient noise to alert her to his arrival outside her door, which worked, because she pulled it open before he had time to knock. Her suitcase was packed and Luc eyed it with loathing.

'You said you'd drive me over to Mum's, but if you've changed your mind...'

'And what? Decided to keep you here under lock and key?'

Agatha didn't say anything. Her silence was even more unwelcome than her spirited arguing and irrational accusations: those he could deal with.

'So have you decided not to talk to me?' he ground out, heaving the suitcase off the bed as though it weighed not much more than a feather, and then half-jogging down the stairs to wait for her at the bottom. A weird, restless energy was pumping through him, making him feel as though he was uncomfortable in his own skin.

'How long will it take to get to Mum's?'

'Long enough. Several hours. I'll make stops along the way so you can stretch your legs.' He was beginning to see which way the wind was blowing and he was liking it less and less. So, personal conversation was off-limits—well, that was fine. He needed a bit of silence to think anyway.

But, after nearly three hours, the silence was as oppressive as a pair of handcuffs in a prison cell. She stared out of the window, lost in her own thoughts. On the two occasions when they had stopped at the services to stretch their legs, she had headed for the newsagent's, not bothering to look back. She had returned with an armful of magazines and some bottled water, and then settled in for the long haul with apparent fascination in the lives of the marginally rich and not-so famous, while he had glared at the road and determinedly tried to engage her in conversation, with no success.

Only when they were finally manoeuvring the familiar streets of their home town did she tear her attention away from the magazines, which she could barely make out in the darkness, and her MP3 player. She had jammed the headphones into her ears, thereby establishing that conversation was out of the question.

'What are you going to tell your mother?' It was the first time the silence had been broken in over forty-five minutes, when he had asked her how she was feeling and Agatha had shrugged and said nothing.

She was as tense as a piece of elastic stretched to breaking point and terrified of being lulled into conversation with him. He was too witty, too sexy, too engaging and far too single-minded for her. Just being in the car with him, knowing that she was being ferried to the safety of her mother's home, made her feel sick with tension. She had hardly given a moment's thought to what lay ahead. She had been too busy trying to deal with what lay right here in the present.

'I don't know,' she reluctantly conceded, her eyes skittering towards his harsh, forbidding profile and then skittering away again just as quickly. 'The truth.'

'It's always a good beginning.'

'Mum's going to be disappointed,' Agatha couldn't help saying with a catch in her voice. She rested one hand on her stomach and tried not to dwell on the disappointment angle. She and her mother had always been united against the world, since her dad had died. How was this going to sit with a woman of essentially old-fashioned values? Like a poisoned apple, she predicted.

'You underestimate people.'

'You don't know Mum.'

'I know her well enough. She's not made of glass, and she's not unaware that accidents happen.' He turned to her, pathetically relieved that she was now, at least, talking. God, he wanted her to smile. He missed that. He missed *her*, even when she was right here, sitting next to him, and it was a missing that was physical. He wondered how it was that he could ever have constructed his life around the loss of a woman who, it now turned out, had been little more than an insignificant interference in his life. Miranda had left him with a jaded palate, but her importance had been greatly exaggerated. He couldn't even remember what she looked like. Had he conclusively blown it with Agatha? He refused to entertain the notion.

They pulled into the drive to her mother's house after a very long and tedious journey and Agatha glanced at him, her hand on the door handle.

'Thanks for the ride.'

'You're not getting rid of me that quickly'

Agatha wished that he just wouldn't look at her like that, with that half-smile of his that could melt every bone in her body. Was he doing it on purpose? 'I guess you want to be a gentleman to the end and bring the bags in for me?' she returned with a tight smile and an edge of bitterness in her voice. But she didn't want to wait and hear confirmation of that, so instead she rustled in her bag for the door key which she had kept and then changed her mind at the last minute and rang the doorbell instead.

There was no chance her mother would be out and, sure enough, after only a few minutes she heard the rustling of footsteps, then a tentative face peered through the peephole in the door and registered the caller with a broad smile. Warm, welcoming arms were outstretched to embrace her the second the door was open.

'You didn't tell me that you were coming down, Aggy. What a treat! Come in, darling. If you'd said, I would have cooked you something special!' Edith was small and round, with short fair hair as flyaway as her daughter's and the same bright blue eyes. When she smiled, there were the ghosts of dimples in her cheeks.

'Mum…'

'Let me look at you!'

'Mum, I've come with, um, Luc—Danielle's son? He kindly gave me a lift here.' Propelled into the hallway, Agatha turned desperately to Luc for support, only belatedly realising how natural this instinct had become for her. He reassured her. She had handed him the power to become her backbone. She couldn't even begin to think how long it would take for her to grope her way back to some sort of independence.

'We're both here for a reason.' Luc placed his arm firmly around Agatha's shoulders and Edith's eyes rounded with surprise.

Agatha, feeling the lazy weight of his arm around her, stiffened in shock. She smiled weakly at her mother, whose eyes were darting curiously between the two of them.

'Reason?' Edith asked, bewildered.

'Ideally, my mother should be here as well, but we'll be breaking the news to her very shortly.'

'News?' Edith and Agatha parroted with varying degrees of stunned surprise.

'Darling.' He leant towards Agatha and she felt his warm breath on her skin. 'Would you like to tell your mother about our news…?'

This wasn't how Agatha had hoped to break it to her mother that she was going to be a grandma but without the ideal scenario of the perfect son-in-law. Cups of tea and a sitting position had been on the agenda but, thrown in the deep end, she managed to splutter, 'I'm, eh, going to have a baby, Mum…' She could feel the heat in her burning face and she couldn't meet her mother's eyes.

'And that's not all.' At last, the words that had eluded

him finally came to his rescue and everything settled into its rightful place. Not everything in life could be controlled; he accepted that and wouldn't have had it any other way. 'I am the very proud father and we're going to be married just as soon as the formalities are worked out...'

There might have been no fainting fit. In fact, the screech from her mother's lips had contained pure joy.

But he had put her in an impossible position and now, with her mother on the telephone tripping over her words to tell Danielle the glad tidings, Agatha finally turned to face him, white-faced and furious.

'How *could* you?' she nearly wept, walking into the sitting room on shaky legs and slumping onto the chair closest to the fireplace.

Luc took a deep breath and moved towards her, gracefully lowering himself to one bended knee and resting his elbow on the side of her chair,

'Look at me. I'm on my knees for you.'

'Stop it!'

'I can't. You do this to me. You bring me to my knees.'

'Don't joke. It's cruel,' Agatha whispered, risking a look at him.

'I wouldn't know how to joke about something like this. I know you think you were lied to over the house, and I'm sorry. And I know you think I took you there so that I could have my wicked way with you, and you're right—I did. I wanted to weld you to me and I just happened to pick the most stupid way of achieving that goal. I didn't stop to think about why it hurt so much when you weren't in my life. I didn't stop to think how it was that I couldn't get you out of my mind. I just knew that I didn't want you to have the freedom you kept harping on about.'

'I didn't want us to be together for the wrong reasons. And I didn't harp on about it.'

'You didn't have to. You said it once and it was enough to bring me out in a cold sweat.'

'But—' her voice trembled '—you don't love me.'

'My life was under control. How was I to know that falling in love would feel like the equivalent of being hit by a lorry? I always figured that love would be as controllable as every other aspect of my life. Then along you came, and half the time I no longer recognised myself. The first time you went away...' Luc's fabulous eyes glittered with emotion. 'I really made the mistake of thinking that things would revert back to normal. I would return to being the working machine I always had been, find another woman, begin the cycle all over again. How hard could it be? You were right when you said that the only lesson I learned from Miranda was how to become an island. I've only now woken up to the fact that being an island isn't what I want to be. I've also realised that I never loved her. I never knew what love was until you came along.'

Agatha found that she was holding her breath just in case this was all a wonderful dream and that blinking too much or breathing too hard would result in her having to wake up.

'Was it...hard?' she whispered, eager for the details, and he gave her a wry smile.

'You're enjoying this, aren't you?'

'No! Yes...Okay...a lot.' She stroked the side of his face and thought that she might just burst with happiness. 'I never thought you'd ever love me. When we broke up, I just decided that I had to get over you and get on with my life, and then I found out that I was pregnant...'

'And I asked you to marry me.'

'And I turned you down,' Agatha murmured ruefully,

thinking how much misery and heartbreak could have been saved had she only known how he felt about her, then blissfully thinking about how much joy and happiness lay ahead. 'I just couldn't imagine marrying you when you didn't love me. I thought ahead to a time when you'd begin to resent the ring on my finger and start hating me for having tied you down with a baby you never asked for.'

'I may not have asked for a baby,' Luc growled with such loving tenderness in his eyes that her heart sang. 'But when you told me that you were pregnant… Put it this way, I got used to the idea in record time, and just as quickly I knew that I wasn't going to let you go again. When you turned me down, I was determined not to let it get in the way of having you. I played on the importance of the baby having a father for all it was worth, and believe me when I tell you that you were never going to a single mother in search of a suitable husband. The only husband you were going to have was *me*.'

'So you sneaked off and bought me the perfect house.'

'I figured, how could you resist a house like that? Ergo, how would you be able to resist *me*? It may have looked conniving to you but it was just my clumsy way of trying to show you that I intended to stay in your life. I should have found the words to say so, but I…didn't know how.'

'You are the most determined guy I've ever met in my entire life, and I'm so glad you are,' Agatha breathed with heartfelt emotion.

'I put my life on hold, pretty much,' Luc confessed, his expressive face darkening. 'And weirdly I enjoyed it. I was out of step with the rest of the world, but I found that, as long as I had you in my sights, I couldn't have given a damn—and then you found the estate agent's brochure and everything blew up in my face.'

'Let's not dwell on that,' Agatha said anxiously. 'I just

love you so much and I just want to hear you tell me that you love me.'

'Isn't that what I've spent the past half an hour doing? Hmm? I love you. Madly. And if we didn't happen to be under your mother's roof...'

There was no need for him to continue the speculation because Agatha knew exactly what he meant and it sent a thrill of anticipation rushing through her like an injection of adrenaline.

'But we're here,' he said with a hungry, possessive look in his eyes. 'And, before your mother comes back in, tell me that you'll marry me and I haven't shot my mouth off for nothing.'

'What do you think, my dearest love?'

Luc did not let the grass grow under his feet. Within three weeks they were married in a quiet but beautiful ceremony surrounded by family and friends. The house which he had cunningly bought as a ploy to win her over became their main residence, with Luc finally admitting defeat and recognising that the only times he really felt truly alive were the times when he was with her. All those domestic values which he had previously abhorred he now embraced, with an alacrity that brought a smile to Agatha's lips and a resigned but contented shrug from him.

'We'll see how long that will last when there's a screaming baby in the house,' she teased him as she grew bigger with her pregnancy, laughing when he fussed over her, even though after the initial poor beginning she proceeded to thrive.

But when Daisy Louise was born two days shy of her due date, an apple-faced cherub with her mother's big blue eyes and her father's thatch of dark hair, Luc proved himself a force to be reckoned with. He had always given one-hundred percent to every single thing he had ever set out to do, and he poured the same unfailing enthusiasm into fatherhood.

He had been gifted a miracle, he smugly told Agatha, and their daughter was destined to achieve every superlative he could think of.

'Don't you want to try for another beautiful miracle?' he murmured lazily, looking at her in a way that could still make her bones melt.

Agatha, having forsaken her job in London in favour of opening a small landscaping concern with two of the mums she had met in the village, resisted for precisely six months. Second time round, her pregnancy was stress free and trouble free, and between Luc and her mother—who was a devoted grandmother and apt to sing the praises of her son-in-law to all and sundry—she was spoiled rotten.

But no passage of time could diminish the love they felt for one another.

She was, to Luc, the very breath of his life. And, well, for Agatha? Who ever said that fairy tales couldn't come true?

MODERN

THE RELUCTANT DUKE
by Carole Mortimer

Forced to return to his family's seat, Lucan St Claire takes beautiful PA Lexie Hamilton with him. Lucan, however, has no idea that his new assistant isn't quite what she seems…

THE DEVIL WEARS KOLOVSKY
by Carol Marinelli

Swearing revenge on the Kolovskys, who abandoned him, Zakahr Belenki determines to destroy their fashion empire! Then he meets his secretary, Lavinia. Her honesty and passion for her job make Zakahr's conscience waver—and inflame his desire…

PRINCESS FROM THE PAST
by Caitlin Crews

Marriage to Prince Leo Di Marco was no fairytale, so Bethany Vassal ran away, hoping the man she loved would come and find her. Now the time has come for Leo to produce a royal heir— and Bethany must return to the castle whence she fled!

INTERVIEW WITH A PLAYBOY
by Kathryn Ross

Marco Lombardi *hates* journalists. Whisking reporter Isobel Keyes away in luxury seems like damage limitation—until she sparks his interest. Now Marco *wants* to kiss and tell…

On sale from 4th February 2011
Don't miss out!

2 FREE BOOKS
AND A SURPRISE GIFT

We would like to take this opportunity to thank you for reading this Mills & Boon® book by offering you the chance to take TWO more specially selected books from the Modern™ series absolutely FREE! We're also making this offer to introduce you to the benefits of the Mills & Boon® Book Club™—

- **FREE home delivery**
- **FREE gifts and competitions**
- **FREE monthly Newsletter**
- **Exclusive Mills & Boon Book Club offers**
- **Books available before they're in the shops**

Accepting these FREE books and gift places you under no obligation to buy, you may cancel at any time, even after receiving your free books. Simply complete your details below and return the entire page to the address below. You don't even need a stamp!

YES Please send me 2 free Modern books and a surprise gift. I understand that unless you hear from me, I will receive 4 superb new books every month for just £3.30 each, postage and packing free. I am under no obligation to purchase any books and may cancel my subscription at any time. The free books and gift will be mine to keep in any case.

Ms/Mrs/Miss/Mr _____ Initials _____

Surname _____

Address _____

_____

_____ Postcode _____

E-mail _____

Send this whole page to: Mills & Boon Book Club, Free Book Offer, FREEPOST NAT 10298, Richmond, TW9 1BR